AMANDA PR

Amanda Prantera was born and educated in England, where she studied philosophy as a research student at London University. She now lives in Rome and is married with two daughters. PROTO ZOË is her fifth book following her novels STRANGE LOOP, THE CABALIST, CONVERSATIONS WITH LORD BYRON ON PERVERSION, 163 YEARS AFTER HIS LORDSHIP'S DEATH and, most recently, THE SIDE OF THE MOON.

sceptre

Amanda Prantera

PROTO ZOË

First published in Great Britain in 1992 by Bloomsbury Publishing Ltd

Sceptre edition 1993

Sceptre is an imprint of Hodder and Stoughton Paperbacks, a division of Hodder and Stoughton Ltd

Printed and bound in Great Britain for Hodder and Stoughton Paperbacks, a division of Hodder and Stoughton Ltd, Mill Road, Dunton Green, Sevenoaks, Kent TN13 2YA. (Editorial Office: 47 Bedford Square, London WC1B 3DP) by Clays Ltd, St Ives plc.

British Library C.I.P.

A CIP catalogue record for this title is available from the British Library

ISBN 0-340-58125-5

FOR CONNIE

CONTENTS

1

Mr Friedmann

On the first Thursday of every month my grandmother and her faithful *doppelgänger* Alice, once lady's maid but now co-militant and companion of the heart, would buckle on their armour and disappear for a day of combat. They were members of a volunteer nursing organization, and their twin stars were rising fast on the County horizon, but positions had to be held and defended. On the Wednesday evening Alice would resurrect her old skills, brush their uniforms speckless, starch their coifs, polish the many medals and badges until they shone so that they hurt the eye, then she would lay out everything on the bed in the room that had once been my grandfather's dressing-room – a severer and more warlike setting than my grandmother's boudoir – and the next morning, after a fortifying bowl of junket and All-bran, the pair of

3

them would be off. Rustling, resolute, their heads held high and dignified despite the erratic starting habits of the Morris Oxford.

This particular Thursday I did not get up to watch them leave, but listened from my bed, stretching my toes and savouring my content. These days were splendid days in my grandmother's household. The cook, usually grumpy in the mornings and attentive only to the Aga and its caprices, would be sitting chatting to the two cleaning-ladies over a cup of tea when I came down for breakfast. She would let me have what I liked, where I liked: fried bread in the sun-porch, or buttered eggs in the kitchen, perched on the new American revolving stool, in the thick of the conversation. I would be allowed to poke my nose into the spice-cupboard where the raisins and sultanas were stored, and perhaps even be granted the ultimate luxury of a quick read of the comic-strips in the *Daily Graphic* or a couple of rounds of whist before work started (it was known I never ratted to my grandmother on these violations of her rules). There would be an atmosphere of happy and relaxed connivance, of feet-on-the-fender and stays-off and hair-down and soused-bloaters-for-lunch; of truancy almost.

Not that my grandmother was disliked by her staff, quite the opposite: it was generally agreed that she was a very good and considerate employer. Not that Alice was unpopular either; her rise was meteoric but no one doubted she had deserved it, and no one envied it her in the least. Quite understandably. But I think that the two of them together, taken punctually day after day after day, like a medicine that is always beneficial, always bracing, always a trifle bitter on the tongue, were simply of too heavy a moral calibre for the average person to bear. They commanded respect, admiration, even genuine affection, but their monthly absences came to the rest of us like oxygen to the stifled. The house breathed when they left and expanded its rib cage with a great satisfied creak, and then breathed again, faster and faster, and bubbled and fizzled, and burped and laughed and grew quite high. And all in a state of more or less total innocence.

On this particular day of deliverance, then, I lay still and warm under the blankets and contemplated the nine or ten hours that lay ahead (perhaps twelve if we were lucky, because today's venue was a distant one), rolling them out before me like a bolt of beautiful soft velvet and relishing the texture.

Unpunctuality being one of the chief enjoyments, I did not stir until an hour or so later, when I heard the noise of a second car crunching up the gravel on the drive. Could it be my grandmother and Alice coming back again to pick up something they had forgotten? Unlikely, they never forgot anything. But still, it was best to make sure: I didn't want to be caught in my nightdress at the ungodly hour of a quarter past nine with the forbidden strains of *Housewives' Choice* blaring out of my bedside radio.

I went to the window and looked down. It was not my grandmother's car. It was not the butcher's

van either, or the milkman's, or the newsagent's, or
the foreman's Landrover, or any other vehicle I was
familiar with. Although, being quite interested in these
things at the time, I knew its make. It was a Lancia
(which I pronounced 'Landseer', like the painter, but
which I was shortly to be put right about). A long,
elegant, dark-green Lancia; a fairly recent model so far
as I could make out, although I knew my books on the
subject were not up to date. Saloon. Four-seater. Big
engine – three litres, maybe bigger. A crack car, what
the gardener's son, who was responsible for forming my
taste in this sphere would have called a lovely piece of
work, and my grandmother a mistake.

I watched as it drew up in front of the main
door, plumb beneath my window. From the chauf-
feur's side, which I soon realized must in fact be the
owner's side because this was the sort of car there
was no point in buying unless you drove it yourself,
a man got out. At least I reckoned he must be a
man, although all I could see of him was the round
of his straw hat and the tips of his shiny pointed
shoes protruding from under its brim. He stood for
a moment – looking about him, I supposed, because
I saw the hat turn pretty well a full circle. Then I
saw the swing of a cane from under the brim, and
heard the bell ring in one long precise ring which
admitted no ignoring, and the steps of the housekeeper
clattering down the stairs to answer it: my grandmother,
amongst her many other scepticisms, did not believe in
carpeting.

I dressed quickly, not without a feeling of irritation. This natty, alien presence might well have come to spoil my day. The man had some kind of business or dealings with my grandmother, that was obvious, there was no one else in the neighbourhood who could command such an exotic caller; he would probably go away therefore when he learnt that she was out. But what if the visit was a social one, and what if he didn't go away? When staying with her I had few household duties imposed on me by my grandmother, but the looking after and entertaining of guests during her absence was one of them, and it was mandatory as it was sacred. 'You are the daughter of the house, Zoë, remember. You must always look after visitors, always be polite to them and see that they have everything they need.' I am not sure she didn't actually lay her hands on my head when she said these words. Anyway, there was no shirking, and nothing to be done but to grit my teeth and carry out her orders. Breakfast in the kitchen was probably off already, because the visitor would want coffee or some other kind of refreshment, and I would have to sit with him while he took it, but perhaps by ten or so he would be gone, and I could get on with my holiday.

By ten o'clock Mr Friedmann (such was the visitor's name) had not departed, and was in fact showing every sign of settling in for the day, but my misgivings on his account had wafted away like thistledown. A god of some kind had clearly come to visit us. A god of fun, and wisdom, and delight. From the moment I walked down the stairs, to be greeted at the bottom by a bow on his part and a seriously executed hand-kiss as if I were a cardinal or an opera singer, I knew that I was in the presence of somebody very special indeed. A being, let us say, of great discernment, capable of recognizing under my seven-and-a-half-year-old exterior, clad in shrunken school jersey and hand-me-down boy's grey flannel trousers from my cousins, the great and fascinating beauty of whose existence to date only I had seemed aware.

Nor was I the only one to come under the spell. In three minutes flat Mr Friedmann had transformed the house into a kind of magic palace of amusements, and all its inhabitants into queens or empresses. No, something in his attitude towards me told me *I* was the sovereign: into princesses, then, or into gracious almost equally important ladies-in-waiting. Please, he wouldn't dream of upsetting our household routine, of putting anybody out in any way. What were we about to do when he had interrupted us? To eat breakfast all together in the kitchen? What a magnificent idea, eggs were always better when they came piping hot off the cooker. Coffee too, he knew all about coffee; ideally coffee should never travel more than three arms' lengths from the stove to the mouth. It was like certain types of wine, nectar in the vat, lizzard-spit when brought to the table. What could be a nicer place to eat breakfast too, he would like to know, than this exquisitely kept and orderly kitchen, clearly presided over by a true artist in the field? Let him see, now. What was this simmering in this delicious-smelling pot here? Stock? No, away with this English modesty! This was bouillon and one of the best and most imaginatively concocted bouillons he had ever come across. Turkey bones – a brilliant addition, but the marjoram – ah, a touch of authentic genius. Look at those copper pans, too, the shine they had got on them. Look at the floor, how impeccably it had been waxed. No, no, having seen this lovely sunny welcoming room, with its (a drawing together of his glossy little shoes here and courteous bows all round) even lovelier and sunnier inhabitants, he would not dream of drinking his coffee anywhere else. Not even if Mr Attlee in person ordered him to do so.

The cook, who to my knowledge had never allowed a house-guest into her domain before and treated even my grandmother as an interloper on those rare occasions she crossed the divide, was at first too shaken to protest, and then, like the rest of us, too swiftly captivated to recall her outrage. Mr Friedmann spoke of the sun flooding the room on a natural basis, but really it was more as if he had brought it with him. The kitchen was my favourite part of the house and always had been, but I could never remember it looking so cheerful, so bright, so inviting as it did then, with that strange little man dancing around in it scattering high spirits like flu germs. Even the housekeeper, who normally took her meals in a room of her own just to distance herself a little from the kitchen staff, seemed unable to resist the allure and joined us at the table.

And when, a little later on, Mr Friedmann spotted the pack of cards under the flour-sieve, and, on being told their purpose, revealed himself anxious above all things to be initiated into the mysteries of contract whist – 'A game I have always yearned to be able to play, dear ladies, but always feared was beyond me' – the sun he had brought with him reached its zenith and we basked in it all of us, taking turns to act as instructress and to sit beside him and help him sort his cards and play his hand.

At some point in this morning of bewitchments the call of duty must have made itself felt in the reluctant hearts of the four lesser princesses, because, exactly how and when I do not remember, eventually I found myself alone with Mr Friedmann, on the other, non-service side of the heavy green-baize door which acted as my grandmother's pale. Sole recipient of his flattering and ego-cosseting attention.

If earlier, in the kitchen, I had basked in the rays of his portable sun, now I wallowed in them, gloried in them. I had occasionally been granted notice from adult visitors before, but had always detected its underpinnings: usually social unease (small children are wrongly thought to be less critical), or else a desire to impress my elder relatives and to reach them through me. With Mr Friedmann there was none of this. His mind did not bend down towards mine – it met it head on in a clash of happy sparks. Lunch I hardly remember eating, although at some time I suppose the cook must have provided us with something – she would have hardly let slip the opportunity for further contact with her hero. But no, following the rapturous overture in the kitchen in concert, all I remember is a sustained duet between the two of us, with no low notes to it, no discords, no loss of rhythm, lasting the entire day.

Mr Friedmann had lived with the Indians in Canada. In the remotest, and thus according to him most Indo-Canadian part of the garden, he taught me tracking and hunting, and how to lay a trail of secret messages in your wake by notching feathers and planting them in a special way in the ground. He held my hands for me while I did this so that I would not hurt myself, and helped me store the spare feathers in the elastic of my knickers, flattened against the curve of the groin so that they would remain uncrushed. There was a whole alphabet of signals to be memorized and stored away and the game was a long one, but I cannot remember it palling on either of us in the slightest; we merely stopped because Mr Friedmann had meanwhile thought of something else.

He had ridden cattle in rodeos in Australia, and going down on all fours to play the part of the steer, he showed me which bits of the animal to cling on to in order to remain in the saddle and which bits to avoid. The skin across the neck was treacherous, he said, it looked a safe bet but in fact it was loose and fat-lined and stretchy and you could be half-way under the belly before you knew where you were. Better to grab hold lower down: there, and there, and – yes, that's right – even there.

Although terrific while it lasted, this game we did not continue playing for quite as long as the first one, for being a proficient rider I learnt the strategic anchoring-places very quickly and developed a crafty way of hooking my fingers into the hide which Mr Friedmann said he thought would work well enough on cattle, perhaps, but *only* on cattle.

He had driven in a famous and dangerous car-race called the Mille Miglia. Towards evening, when the gardener started up the mowing machine close by and you could no longer pretend you were in the outbacks of anywhere, so much noise did it make, Mr Friedmann helped me into his car beside him and showed me what it had been like; letting me sit in his lap on the driving side and actually manoeuvre the wheel and slide my feet on to the pedals. It was quite easy when you got the hang of it: down quickly, clutch-and-accelerator-and-clutch with the tips of your toes as if you were dancing, and then slither up again fast between the friendly fork of Mr Friedmann's legs to shift the gear-lever into place. Holding the wheel steady, of course, all the time. I remember at one point asking to be allowed to use the horn too, to bring the gardener's boy running and flaunt my good luck under his nose: I knew he'd have given anything to sit at the wheel of a car like that, even stationary as we were now. But Mr Friedmann explained to me that you do not hoot your horn while racing if you can help it, the whole point being to creep up behind your adversaries and whoosh past them when they are least expecting it.

This reasoning made sense, but I was sorry to have no witnesses to my moment of glory, and very pleased therefore when I saw the face of the housekeeper looking out of the dining-room window at us, her eyes suitably wide with surprise. At least I would not now be accused of fibbing. I waved at her energetically, to show that I had noticed being noticed.

The car-race sadly turned out to be our last game, and we didn't even finish it properly as it was. Mr Friedmann seemed to tire of it suddenly for some reason – perhaps my waving so hard had broken the thread of his concentration – and you must never drive when you are tired, he said, you must get straight out of the car and make for a quiet, out-of-the-way spot where you can rest. We had just transferred ourselves to the wine-cellar (the most out-of-the-way spot I could think of at such short notice), and Mr Friedmann had just begun to show me some of his mining adventures in Colorado, using the convenient darkness of the cellar to simulate the mine, when we were reached by a rather flustered-looking housekeeper, who had evidently sought us in vain on the hastily abandoned track of the Mille Miglia and perhaps several other places as well, to tell me it was bed-time.

I went unprotesting: we all knew this was the one point on which it would be folly to disobey my grandmother's orders. Young as I was I think I already knew too that perfection, to remain perfection, must be finite, and that the raw, truncated endings that grown-ups put to things were usually the right ones. I remember no sadness, therefore, on leaving my new companion, merely a quick pang of disappointment as the mine he had created in our joint imagination was turned back into a cellar again by the sudden switching on of the electric light, and a faint twinge of irritation at the housekeeper for being so very brusque in the way she packed me off. I thought, given the fun she had had at cards with him that morning, that she owed it to Mr Friedmann to be a bit more smiley in his presence.

For the rest, I was buoyant, enraptured, untouchable in my cocoon of happiness. I lay in my bath and in the flickering of the late summer sunlight on the ceiling above contemplated the beatific vision of the first truly perfect day of my life. I ate my supper in a whirl of mines and rodeos and race-tracks, giddy with the idea of how many wonderful things the world had in store for me. I went to bed, the sun still high, and my grandmother still not back from her campaigning (it looked as if Mr Friedmann had given up waiting for her too, because when I peeped out of the window the 'Lancha' – that was how you pronounced it, 'Lancha' – was no longer to be seen), and fell asleep immediately, coiled over my happiness like a boa. My grandmother had a way of taking things away from you if she thought you were fond of them – *over*fond of them, as she put it – but this one was already safe inside me in the past, this one she would not lay her hands on.

The next day, when I went down to breakfast, it was to the sober routine of always. My happiness was still very much with me, but I carried it like a toper his bottle, careful not to let it show. My grandmother was already at table, opening her post with a mournful look, her shoulders already braced for the cares of the day to drop on them – when they had not already dropped, as today it seemed they had.

If I had expected sternness from her, though, or cross-examination, as was usual when I had spent a day outside the radius of her vigilance, I was wrong. She watched me, it was true, unusually closely even for her, hardly taking her eyes off me for the entire meal, but she did so with great sweetness and tenderness. Not the way she did when she thought I had been up to mischief or gadding around enjoying myself more than was advisable, but the way she did when I was ill.

It was only with the arrival of the stewed prunes that she spoke, and then in a low and gentle voice, filled with concern.

'Did you have a nice day yesterday, Zoë, while I was away?'

Striving for a perfect balance between carelessness and candour I replied that yes, thank you very much, Grandmother, I did.

'Nothing happened . . . ?' She choked over her prunes and a stone shot out of her mouth in a clumsy way I had never associated with her before. 'Nothing unpleasant happened which you would like to tell me about?'

Here was the cue for innocent surprise mixed with another dash of carelessness. 'Nothing,' I said. 'Nothing I can remember. Why?'

'Oh, no reason,' my grandmother said awkwardly – she was a less-gifted actress than myself when it came to light-comedy roles. 'I just thought . . . all on your own like that . . . But then you weren't on your own all the time, were you? You were with . . . ' She paused and I saw her tighten her grip on the spoon until her knuckles shone, but whether her firmness was for me or the prunestones I could not tell, 'Mr . . . er . . . What was the man's name? Mr Friedmann.'

'Yes, Grandmother.'

Still the hand holding the spoon remained clenched. 'And was he kind to you, this Mr Friedmann?'

'Very,' I said, in my best throwaway style. 'Very kind, very nice. He taught me . . . ' I corrected myself, I wanted no trace of my true enjoyment to show through in case she noticed the shine. 'He told me a lot of interesting things.'

The skin on her knuckles appeared to relax a little. 'About, my sweet?'

Vagueness was what was needed here. Perhaps even a tiny speck of boredom. 'Oh, about Indians, and machines, and mining and things,' I said. 'Things like that.'

The spoon fell from my grandmother's grasp, ringing on the table noisily, but she did not seem to notice it. 'Well,' she said, picking up her letters with a sigh, but not a careworn one this time, more of a sigh of relief, 'Well, then, that's all I wanted to know really, if you had had a nice day. And it was? You're sure it was, are you? Every moment of it?'

I nodded emphatically, my face held up for inspection, clear and shining like a mirror in the sun.

'Well,' she said again, her attention now beginning to shift back more markedly towards her correspondence, 'then when you've finished breakfast you can run along. Mind you stay close to the house, though. I never again want you straying far from the house. Neither on your own, nor with anyone else. Do you understand?'

I understood in part. My grandmother knew something, suspected something about the riotous, wholly inappropriate way I had spent my day, but for some reason best known to herself she was not going to take me up on it. Even though she had, so to speak, caught a glimpse of it out of the corner of her eye and sensed its pagan shape and gaudy brightness, she was going to let me keep this particular nugget of happiness to myself. And that was all that mattered.

Let *us* keep it to *our*selves, that is, because the treasure was fortunately a shared one: one that could be taken out of its cache when you were between friends, and unwrapped and turned over and over and admired, and talked about until you were tired of talking. In fact I wasn't sure that this wasn't going to be the best part of all – just going over things together and remembering. Freed from my grandmother's scrutiny at last, I crashed through the green-baize door to the side of my allies and zoomed into the kitchen like an aeroplane, my arms spread wide, babbling as I came.

'Will he be back one day soon, do you think, our Mr Friedmann?' I asked, plonking myself down on the revolving stool for a quick spin and addressing my question to the back of the cook, who was alone there, her attention already totally reclaimed by her taskmaster the Aga. 'Oh, I do hope so, don't you? Oh, wasn't he nice! Wasn't he super! Didn't we have fun! Do you remember the froth on the coffee and how he did it? And the parsley moustache? And the quiz about the dead man and the bed? Do you remember the face he made when you took that trick of his with that little trump, and he . . . '

I stopped short. The cook had wheeled round as if placed on a revolving stool herself, and was staring at me like a stranger, her face deformed by some terrible emotion. I identified it immediately as hatred, although how I put a name to it so swiftly I don't know, I don't think I had ever seen hatred before.

'Don't you name that name in here!' she spat at me. 'Don't you ever name that name again! He's *not* a nice man, he's a horrible, foul, disgusting man, and the sooner you get that into your head the better! We never want to hear him mentioned again, any of us. As far as we're concerned we never set eyes on him. Little rat, little sneaking rat come up from the sewers, let him go back there where he belongs!' And she spun round to the Aga again, leaving me so shocked, so utterly

18

confused and broken that I could do nothing, not even move away.

I waited for tears to come and release me. And when they came I ran. Where I ran to I do not remember exactly, but I have a feeling that it was to the wine-cellar. If so, then presumably the idea was to catch hold of something of Mr Friedmann there – some scrap, some trace of his presence – and stow it away somewhere secret before it too disappeared or was torn from me by treachery.

The lesson I learnt from this sad little episode – or let us say the result it led to; you can hardly speak of learning when for years on end I steadfastly refused to think about anything connected with the matter – was merely this: that from that day on, when staying with my grandmother I played my outdoor games closer to the house as requested, gave up contract whist in favour of bridge, and spent more and more time when I was not outdoors on what I had formerly considered the wrong side of the green-baize door but now began to look on as the right one. I never formulated the thought to myself, but inside me I think I had unconsciously begun to subscribe to the opinion, often voiced by my grandmother and her circle of friends, that the working classes were fundamentally disloyal and unreliable. They couldn't help it, poor things, and Alice of course was an exception, but that was the way they were made.

2

Gigli Sings

I had another grandmother, of course, a more frivolous and less committed one, but I was not encouraged to think of her as a grandmother. In fact both by her and her formidable counterpart, although for widely different reasons, I was encouraged to look on her as a fairly distant relation of a generation closer to my own and to call her Catkin. Her name was Catherine, and in the half-light she was always careful to set about her she looked not a day over forty, so the nickname was not inappropriate.

I never spent much time with this other grandmother, nor she with me, which seemed to suit us all very well: she confessed freely to a horror of 'ankle biters', and was always busy abroad, pursuing elusive forms of artistic expression such as oil-painting, or memoir-writing, or simply and less specifically 'surrounding

herself with Beauty' while she played her waiting
game with the recalcitrant Muses. One Easter holidays,
however, my real, dependable grandmother fell ill and
was taken to hospital, and I was packed off, grumbling
and disoriented, to the Italian Riviera to stay with
Catkin in her very grand but at the same time rather
seedy and dilapidated rented villa at Rapallo: the Villa
Azalea, pronounced As-a-layer.

It was not a stay I remember very clearly or willingly,
except for its closing episode, which stands out in my
mind chiefly because my other grandmother, when she
got back from hospital, made me recite it to her over
and over again – all its details – until we both us of
had it virtually by heart. Catkin was into music at the
time and spent most of the day practising at the piano,
or else winding up a huge wooden gramophone and
playing records of famous arias while she mouthed the
words to them in front of the mirror. (Or those words
she could remember: 'Caaaro nome, plim, plim, plim;
caaaro nome, blum, blum, blum. Ve . . . sti la whatsit.
Che gelida manina, se la la la la la la la!') I was left very
much to my own devices, which I normally would
not have minded, but I was on foreign ground and
my devices were few. Once, as a great concession, she
took me to the beach, but even then the gramophone
had to accompany us, and to our mutual agreement the
trip was not repeated.

The Villa Azalea was dank and sparsely furnished,
and uninspiring for a child. Catkin had done her best
to liven it up according to her lights, but her lights

were, as I said, deliberately kept very low, and once the sun had gone down there was scarcely a place in which one could so much as read in any comfort. Not that there was much *to* read, even if I had been able to: literature was in abeyance so far as Catkin was concerned, it was music, music, music, all day long; she was living the season of her musical springtime, or, as she liked to put it, of her own private 'Maggio Musicale', and the other arts were temporarily dismissed as time-wasting and distracting. Twice a week, on Mondays and Thursdays, a music teacher arrived to give her a lesson in the art of *solfeggio*; a meek little man who smelt of rancid butter and fawned over Catkin and called her 'Leddy Caterina', and who lingered on painfully after each lesson until asked to lunch. Twice a week also, although on different days so as not to overstrain her voice, a small group of music-loving friends from nearby villas would be invited to drop in to give life to what I think I heard Catkin quite seriously refer to as her Musical Workshop (and which seemed to me to consist of her singing her head off while one of her guests accompanied her at the piano and another turned the pages, and everyone else sitting there and fidgeting and eyeing the gin bottle which they knew would be passed round afterwards). And on Sundays, exertions over, the same group would reassemble in one or other of the villas for a musical treat provided by a professional performer. Again, from the looks of it, usually laid on and financed by Catkin, and again, from the sound of it, usually rather dull.

I spent probably not more than three and a half weeks, four at the outside, in this dingy, reverberating penumbra, scuffing along the corridors feeling useless, trying to find ways of amusing myself that did not interfere with Catkin's programme or disturb her ear, but to me the weeks dragged like aeons. To my English nerve-ends it was already too hot to sit outside, and anyway, the garden, pared smooth like the interior of the villa for rented occupancy, offered no sources of fun or interest; nothing but dusty grey palm trees and shingle, and a few wretchedly exposed geraniums set out in rows. So I mostly kept inside and kicked my heels in time to Catkin's metronome. I couldn't even talk to the maids, we couldn't understand each other.

Towards the end of my visit, however, when it was almost too late to matter, things suddenly took a turn for the brighter. We were having lunch, Catkin and I – in the pungent company, naturally, of the music teacher because it was a Thursday – when a note was brought in by one of the maids. It came, she announced, from the 'Maggiore'. By which, Catkin said excitedly as she ripped open the envelope with a tuning-fork, was meant Major McDermot, one of her favourite musical cronies, who had quite a bit of leverage in Italian cultural circles and had promised to come up with something really special for her next little 'do'.

The contents of the message – its exact wording, that is – was much discussed afterwards, but the original having been mislaid in the meantime, there was no possibility of carrying out a proper check on the

Major's spelling or punctuation. I was repeatedly cross-examined as to what Catkin had said on reading the note – it was thought somehow that I would prove a more reliable witness than the maid and the music teacher – but, like these other two, all I remembered was Catkin giving a great shriek and uttering the surname: Gigli! as if it was spelt with a dozen e's. (I said I also thought I heard her exclaim, Bugger my boots! and, What a sock in the eye for Frieda! but this did not seem to be considered an important piece of testimony and I was asked to forget it.)

Anyway, the essence of the Major's message was that this Gigli, whoever he was, was coming to sing at Catkin's next musical Sunday, and the news appeared to electrify the entire household. The music teacher, I recall, had tears in his eyes as the truth was confirmed to him; he kept reaching out for Catkin's hand and kissing it, and telling her she was a great benefactress of the arts, and saying, 'Grazie! Grazie!' and then, when Catkin removed her hand as she did pretty smartly, blowing his kisses into the air: Smack! The Maestro! Smack! The Maestro here in person in three days' time, under this very roof! What good fortune! What would his colleagues in the orchestra say when he told them? Smack! Smack! Smack! The maid, less sentimental but also clearly impressed to the marrow, disappeared into the kitchen, from where more excited voices could soon be heard, arguing and chattering and lifting themselves in snatches of song. Songs from opera, of course, in anticipation of the visit. While

Catkin herself, calm and businesslike after her inital outburst, procured pen and paper and began making a list of people to invite to the grand event. She looked smug and slightly vindictive as her pen sped down the page, jotting down and crossing out, and every now and again she would interrupt her scribbling to rub her eyes (perhaps to convince herself she wasn't dreaming) and would say, 'Well, I must say, fancy the Major pulling it off. I never thought, somehow . . . I never imagined . . . Well, well, well,' Or words to that effect.

For the next three days, in fact right up to the moment, at nine o'clock sharp on the Sunday evening when Major McDermot made his perplexing appearance in the sitting-room with the captured celebrity on his arm, the house and all its inhabitants gave off a kind of glow of pride and busy expectancy mixed. Polish glistened on the furniture and floors, sweat shone on the faces of the maids as they polished, and the sunlight, admitted if only briefly for the purpose of cleaning, danced on every surface and made things brighter still.

Caught up in the whirl of preparations I had no time to feel lonely any more, and as for feeling useless – it would have been impossible with all the tasks I was given to carry out. I was sent to the market by Ernesto the cook to buy missing ingredients for the after-recital buffet he was preparing in the Maestro's honour. Nutmeg, I think it was, and truffles which cost a bomb. I was sent by the houskeeper to the woman who did the laundry to recover a pile of much-needed table napkins. (Catkin's guest-list grew longer and longer each day, as she discovered that, friends or enemies alike, there was more satisfaction in inviting than excluding; I could hear her shrilling down the telephone all day, repeating afresh to each guest the magic name, Gigli, Gigli, Gigli, always with the same abundance of e's.) I was sent to the parish with a request for chairs, and from there to the headquarters of the Communist party which had borrowed them for some function or other and never returned them. I was sent to the piano-tuner with a cheque to cover his bill and a letter begging urgently for his services. I was sent for material to hang up on the wall of the drawing-room behind the piano to improve the acoustics. I was sent to the chemist for throat pastilles in case the Maestro needed any. I was shuttled back and forth and left and right until I could hardly stand, I was so tired.

And throughout all the shuttling I was happier than I had ever been – at least since I had set foot on Italian soil. Linked by the common cause, I seemed to be able to understand part of what the maids were saying and could follow snatches of their conversation, even laugh at some of their jokes. The house, filled now with chairs and flowers and smelling quite different, seemed suddenly more welcoming, I felt almost at home in it. Catkin, too, was different – all sweet and smiley and accessible, inviting me into her room for advice on what dress to wear on the evening of the recital, asking me to hold her toes apart while she painted her toenails, behaving to me almost like a sister, or how I imagined a sister would behave. I could feel she no longer resented my presence, in fact she seemed actually glad to have me with her. Altogether, despite the fact that the music was temporarily silent and Catkin had closed her practice books and the metronome had stopped ticking, it was a period of rare harmony between us, rare sunniness.

Which made the storm, when it came, all the blacker. Not that I, thank goodness, was the target of Catkin's rage. Indeed I was so innocent and ignorant of what happened that I'm not sure I really noticed anything much amiss until the morning after the recital, when the analysis of the famous message was attempted. (And even then it took me some time to discover what all the fuss was about, and why Catkin was so anxious to determine where Major McDermot had put his full stops and whether he had indeed printed 'Sig.na', as he swore he had, or 'Sig.', as Catkin swore she had read.) I was, it is true, slightly surprised, when the Major and his star-performer appeared arm-in-arm in the doorway, to see that the celebrated singer Gigli was a woman when I had somehow got it into my head that he was a man, but I reckoned I had just made a mistake and gave no more thought to the matter. After all, singers, male or female, always seemed to go by just their surnames, so how was one to tell? I was also slightly surprised to see Catkin, too, looking surprised: surely, with her knowledge of music, she was one person who did know which sex this Gigli person belonged to and what register he or she sang in? But what Catkin, from under her ice-pack the next day, called the Débâcle, the Fiasco, the Public Disgrace, the Worst Humiliation to which she had Ever Been Subjected – this passed me by altogether. In fact most of the guests were smiling so widely and appearing to enjoy themselves so much, and Miss Gigli sang so bouncily and wolfed down Ernesto's buffet with such zest, I thought the whole evening had been a terrific success.

My other grandmother was a shade disappointed with me for noticing so little. Which is perhaps why she had me repeat the story to her so often: she hoped that more details would come back to me in the telling. 'Try to remember exactly who was there, Zoë' she would urge me. 'The English guests, I mean. And then see if you can remember what their faces looked like during the recital, and what they said afterwards and what they did.' But apart from one or two tiny things, like my spotting Catkin on the terrace, pinning the Major in a corner and grasping him very tightly by his bow-tie until he spluttered, or my hearing the woman that Catkin called Frieda whisper loudly to her neighbour, 'Poor Catherine, what a cropper! I think I'm going to wet my knicks laughing,' I didn't really manage to recall anything of significance, and my grandmother had to be content with the story as it was.

Although content, of course, is not a fair word to use. Often though she made me tell it and willingly though she listened, I think the account truly upset my grandmother on Catkin's behalf, who, after all, was a kind of relation, and as such came under the umbrella of family loyalty. Taking out her handkerchief, she would cover her mouth with it and touch the corners of her eyes as if she had tears in them that needed mopping, and as I reached the end she would invariably echo the words of the Frieda woman (although, naturally, not those regarding the wetting of knicks). 'Poor Catherine,' she would say feelingly through the lace. 'Poor, *poor* Catherine, what a very large cropper indeed!'

3

The Coming of Chamonix

This is no story really, but a disgracefully overdue thank-you letter. To a benefactress I owe much to, but about whom I remember little save for her unforgettable Christian name and the unforgettable good turn she did me, simply by existing and crossing my path when she did. I hope she is well and – from the moment our paths uncrossed again at any rate – has had a happy life, she certainly deserved it.

Many years ago now, you see, when I was eight, my parents sent me to boarding school, and unwittingly to Hell. The road that led to it being in their case truly paved with good intentions. The school was not even a proper school, it was a kind of extended family, run by friends. It catered for a mere fifteen pupils – two of them children of the house. The matron was these children's ex-nanny, the teacher their governess, Miss Tufnell; pupils called them Nanny and Tuffy respectively. In the dormitories, which again were not properly speaking dormitories but guest-bedrooms with added beds, teddy bears and chintzes abounded. You were allowed to bring your own rabbits and guinea-pigs with you and lodge them in special hutches in the kitchen garden. If you had one, and your parents were willing to pay the extra fee for stabling, you could even bring your own pony. It was that kind of set-up. Cosy, welcoming, home from home as my parents repeatedly told me. And for Lucifer I suppose this would have been true.

I brought with me no live animals, thank goodness. My stuffed ones left me vulnerable enough as it was. No sooner had I started unpacking, than they were snatched from the top of my trunk where they were lying and passed scornfully from hand to grubby hand by my new room-mates. What were the names of these revolting objects? Lord, what idiot names! Why didn't I have an ordinary bear like everyone else and call it Teddy? They bet it was because I was a prissie. Hey, give here! Pass it here! This is what we do with rotten animals like these, just watch! And I watched obediently, ignorant as yet of the rules of this particular game, as my beloved leopard Leopold was transfixed on a knitting needle and whirled in the air before me just beyond my grasp, and as his companion, Basil the Badger, disappeared out of the window to a roar of laughter and landed in a puddle below.

I don't think I need bother to describe in detail all the various tortures that followed. School bullying is a well-known phenomenon, largely untouched by fashion, and apart from one or two bright ideas like the above skewering of my leopard, the techniques employed in this case were none of them particularly innovative or noteworthy. I was given apple-pie beds, sometimes wet, sometimes dry, sometimes sugared. I was laughed at for reasons that were never made clear to me. I was quizzed, grilled, cross-examined about my home and family, and my replies broadcast to choruses of guffaws: 'Her father has a Mercedes! Cripes! Uccck! Ugggh! Her mother wears camiknickers! She's allowed to go into the bathroom when her father's having his bath! Uck! Uck! Uck!' I was shunned and harassed by turns; I was kicked in the backside while saying my prayers; I was pinched, I was goaded, I was constantly rebuked for crying, although I never to my knowledge did so, being by then too deeply withdrawn into myself to display any emotion at all. I was lured to do dangerous actions and ignored once I had performed them. In short I was given standard treatment, to which I responded in more or less standard fashion. Save for the fact that I did not, I am quite sure of this, connive or in any way collaborate with my tormentors. I say this because I read recently in some learned book that bullying is – what did they call it? – a dyadic relationship, something of the kind, to which both parties, bully and victim, have to subscribe before it can get under way. In my case it was not so. This just for the record.

What the book also said, though, and this time I think quite correctly, was that the victim is nearly always singled out on the grounds of his or her diversity from the group. And here, of course, despite many and pathetic efforts not to, I fulfilled the condition all too well. Small but undisguisable differences set me apart; signals winked; whiffs of exotic scent beckoned to the hounds to follow and close in. My hair to begin with: frizzy, thick, and acknowledging no Anglo-Saxon compliance to the laws of gravity. My religion, Roman Catholic. Its accoutrements of rosary and missal – two objects again tossed frequently out of the window for me to recover amidst mirth. The weekly attendance at another church in the company of the Irish cook who was the only other Catholic in the place. My parents' marital status: still united while everyone else's were divorced. And above all my clothes.

Oh, my clothes, my clothes! How many times, I wonder, did my letters home contain pleas for sky-blue sweaters from Selfridges and box-pleated navy skirts to be sent to replace the less orthodox wardrobe that Alice and my grandmother had lovingly concocted for me? Rust, moss, old gold, Venetian mauve; velvets in place of tweed and flannel; patterns cut by my grandmother in the style of her revered pre-Raphaelite masters; ambitious stitches, not quite perfectly executed – I could remember the two women's pride when they had shown me their handiwork, and mine too when I had tried it on. Now, the sight of each item as it came back from the wash made me sick with dread at the thought of having to claim it, wear it, and listen to the taunts it would unfailingly attract.

Yes, I think it was my wardrobe that caused me the most anguish. Largely, I suppose, because alone of my strangenesses I could not help realizing that it could with a little less imagination have been avoided. Hair, parents and religion were things that just happened to people and too bad if they happened oddly, but the wretched clothes had been *chosen* – meditated on beforehand and then deliberately foisted on me. There was an element of treachery here connected with my family which I discerned and resented; an element of treachery within myself also for harbouring such resentment. The effects of torture, as the book I mentioned points out, are many and complex and not always linear in their thrust.

How long this state of affairs lasted I do not honestly know, having, as I said, pulled in my antennae more or less entirely in the interests of survival, but I remember suffering agonies on account of a thick felt winter cloak of Peter Pan inspiration (I have the impression its hem was cut jagged like a leaf, and that wet leaves were plastered all over me while I was wearing it, or perhaps placed in my bed later that night), and I remember similar agonies concerning a light muslin smock, again most likely with a Barrie-ish or Rackhamish touch to it, so I presume the ordeal must have lasted at least a year, if not more. I also remember asking one of my chief tormentors to stay with me during one of the holidays, with the intention of winning her round.

This ended in disaster. She became my best and dearest friend for the duration of the holiday, flirted with my father, ingratiated herself with my mother who thought she was wonderful, and then, once we were back at school again, went round telling everyone (oh, that most dreaded of all words: a stave went through my heart when I heard it) that they were a couple of all-time super-prissies, and that my mother wore not only camiknickers but silly hats with veils and my father belched at mealtimes.

It must have been shortly after this débâcle, for I remember that the above story was still going the rounds and I was still being belched at left, right and centre whenever my back was turned (stirring up in me yet more feelings of resentment, because it was true, my father burped like a sea-lion, especially in front of guests, and thought it very funny), when salvation at last arrived. In the unlikely person of a small, blonde-haired, straw-hatted newcomer, brought into the bedroom by Nanny and introduced to us as Chamonix.

For the first few minutes it was unclear to all of us what effects this new arrival would produce. Schooled by now to pessimism, I expected at the best a short respite while the routine questions were asked and the child's belongings inspected, and then most likely an addition to the pack of my persecutors. Chamonix's hair was like spun silk, her appearance neat and unremark-able, her clothes impeccably right. Visually, she fitted in. Nor did the perusal of her suitcases lead to any promising discoveries. Her teddy was a teddy and was called Edmund – only a slight deviation from the norm. Her skirts were grey and dark-blue and pleated, her jerseys bore the right labels, she had pyjamas, not dastardly nighties like I did. So it wasn't until the unpacking was over, and, disappointed by their search, the attention of the other girls began to shift from what there was inside the cases to what there was not, that I began to see, very faint at first, like the glow of a torch held under the bedcovers for secret reading, a ray of light.

Why didn't she have a toothbrush? Chamonix was asked. Had her mother forgotten to pack it? From under the silken fringe the new girl's eyes looked out candidly, trustingly, at her audience. No, she replied, she didn't have a toothbrush – although she did have a hairbrush, look. (The jury looked and nodded: there was nothing to be said, the make was just the same as everybody else's) – but she didn't have a toothbrush because her mother said it was bad for you to brush your teeth, you were better off just eating an apple last thing at night, it was more natural.

There was a slight stirring among the inquisitors and then silence: they did not know how to take this one. I crossed my fingers and prayed to my outlandish God whose interest in my plight until now I had been beginning to doubt. Make her a real prissie, oh, please, Lord, make her a real prissie, I beg.

What did she mean, natural?

Simple said Chamonix, flattered by the attention she was arousing (little did she know what it boded) and starting to pontificate a bit: in keeping with God's plans. If he had wanted us to brush our teeth he would have given us bristly fingers. Just as if he had wanted us to take aspirin when we were ill he would have given us aspirin trees.

Another puzzled silence. Then on the face of the Queen torturer, the one I had invited home with me with such sorry results, a tiny smile of excitement began to appear. She patted the bed invitingly, drawing Chamonix close. For the first time since I myself had undergone the same inquiry my Catholicism and all my other crimes ceased to weigh on me so heavily. In fact my shoulders felt almost light. I walked over to the corner of the room where my own bed was situated, moving quietly, like a recently freed prisoner who still fears his chains will clank, and began to play with my much deteriorated animals. Too early to communicate the good news to them, but the idea had begun to dawn on me that perhaps from now on things were going to look up for all three of us.

My hopes grew as the cross-examination continued. Chamonix, it emerged, was what was called a Christian Scientist. (I imagine now of a particularly strict, perhaps idiosyncratic kind, but anyway, whatever kind, it clearly knocked Roman Catholicism for six.) Toothbrushes and aspirin were not her only taboo, she shunned thermometers and cough syrup and indeed anything to do with medicine, and if a doctor came near her, or so I heard her declare theatrically to the glee of her listeners, she would kill herself rather than let him examine her. She was a vegetarian, whatever that meant, and a pacifist, whatever that meant too: she was not too clear on either head herself save that, again, both things had to do with universal harmony. She had spent last summer in a nudist colony in the South of France – no, it hadn't been disgusting at all: her parents had taught her that the body was beautiful and not a thing to be ashamed of. (Talk about lightness, I felt so ethereal I could have flown: what were my father's belches and easy bathroom habits compared to this?) She did not fear the cold, nor illness for that matter, nor even death, because, faced with any of these all you had to do was sit quietly in a room and read special passages from the works of Mrs Somebody-or-other and things would come right again.

I don't know about this Mrs Whatever-her-name-was's powers, but it seemed my own God had at last got round to using some of his. When I heard one of the girls being sent off into the garden to procure the corpse of a pet rabbit that had died some days earlier, in order that Chamonix's claim might be put to the test, I knew I was almost out of the wood. The circle around the bed where Chamonix was sitting tightened, leaving me in sweet and easeful solitude. It was not, however, until I heard someone ask 'And why are you called Chamonix? What on earth sort of a name is that?' and Chamonix's voice replying, still candidly, still full of misplaced confidence, 'My parents called me Chamonix because it is the name of the place where I was conceived, where my father put the seed in my mother's tummy which turned into me.' It was not until then, when the snorts started up and the howls of derision began to follow, that I bent down to whisper to Leopold and Basil the definitive news of our rescue.

And rescue it was, and definitive also. I spent another two terms in the place, unmolested, unnoticed almost. Frizz, velvets and rosary notwithstanding, thanks to poor Chamonix it was as if I had become invisible.

4

The Sewing Lesson

An unlikely, unDarwinian occupation, maybe, but my grandmother, besides nursing, and supervising (somewhat closer since Mr Friedmann's visit) my holiday education, and hurtling round the countryside with Alice in quest of paramilitary glory, bred horses. Race horses, flat-race horses, of the most superior and delicate kind. What with stallion fees, and mare care, and special gestation fodder, and stabling and veterinary bills, each one of her yearlings cost, even in those cheaper and genetically more insouciant days, thousands of pounds to produce. The rationale behind what would otherwise have been sheer business folly was that at the moment of sale each yearling would then cost someone else even more thousands of pounds to buy *from* my grandmother, but alas this reasoning did not always seem to hold good. As I said, the animals were tricky and delicate, and also remarkably cussed: they had a way of laming themselves (usually only seconds before auction, when it was too late to withdraw them) and at the appointed moment would drag themselves round the parade ring like game but grievous invalids, discouraging all but the wiliest purchasers from making a bid. This, when they did not develop last-minute whooping cough, or kick through the floor of the horsebox and graze their legs to shreds on the tarmac, or glut themselves on some forbidden foodstuff and blow out like horrible equine balloons. Or when they did not choose earlier and more radical options for reciprocal ruin – theirs and my grandmother's – such as contriving to be born dead, or suffocating in the straw shortly afterwards, or impaling themselves on railings, or committing hara-kiri on an upturned hay fork.

Such being the situation, you can well imagine that the foaling season on my grandmother's stud farm was a time of acute tension. Much as it would be, I presume, on a farm of lemmings and for not dissimilar reasons. Each birth was followed like a royal one. Bulletins were issued every half hour or so from what was called the 'sitting-up' room, a room adjacent to the foaling-stable from which the studgroom, vet and foreman, Bovril mugs in hands, could keep vigil through a small hatch in the wall over the mare in labour. These bulletins were then shuttled over to the house by the gardener's son on his bicycle, pink in the face with pride and embarrassment and hurry mixed, and delivered to my grandmother, who also 'sat up' on her own account, straight-backed and silent, inexpertly puffing, in best parent-to-be manner, at a series of Black Sobranie cigarettes, extracted from a special cabinet only on these occasions.

I can remember being deeply troubled by my grand-mother's passivity at such times. Offended too, I think, perhaps even threatened. With her uniforms and medals and general air of authority over everyone and every-thing, I had come to look on her as the embodiment of power. And I had come to think of power itself, in consequence, as a typically female possession. She had it, I was her heir, her direct descendant through the female line (which as all horse-breeders know is the one that really counts), therefore one day it would be mine. The argument was sound and simple and nicely convincing. But to see her in these moments of puerperal crisis, banished from the scene of action by some strange set of rules I did not fully grasp, relegated to her drawing-room where she sat stabbing forlornly with watering eyes at scraps of embroidery while a trio of men in whom I knew she placed scant faith presided over the fortunes of *her* horses, *her* investments, *her* livelihood – well, it made me think again about the power distribution between the sexes, and think in not very reassuring terms.

Nor did the answers to the questions I posed her as I kept her company through some of these lonely, enervating vigils do much to set my mind at rest. If she was so worried about the outcome, I urged her, why didn't she go over to the sitting-up room herself and make sure things were going as they should? Women often delivered babies in films, didn't they? Boiled up water and tied the umbilical cord and things? Well, yes, I was assured quietly, but the birth of a foal was rather different from that of a baby. It was more . . . more raw . . . more violent. It was not the right sort of spectacle for women, or not for certain kinds of women. It was a *coarsening* experience, that was it. Or could be. It was better left to men. Had I ever heard of women being present in the covering-yard when the mating season was on? Of course I hadn't, and for the same reason: there would be nothing wrong in it but it would not be seemly. 'Pas convenable, Zoë, tu comprends?' (And when my grandmother resorted to French it meant the conversation was at an indisputable close.) These were things which, now that I was growing up, I must simply learn to understand.

I did understand, or began to – especially at the mention of the covering-yard, which was a dank, god-forsaken place, so full of whips and twitches and other horsey horrors that no one in their right mind, male *or* female, would ever want to visit it, so far as I could see – but the understanding brought me little comfort. Raw or not, *convenable* or *pas convenable*, there were clearly important areas, no, worse, *vital* areas, of life from which women were excluded. And this, however imaginatively or superciliously you tried to look on it, spelt a lessening of their power. Our power. My power. I was particularly heartened, therefore, when on one of these tense, pre-natal evenings, as my grandmother and

I sat huddled together in the drawing-room pretending busyness with our needles and scanning the horizon like Fatima and Sister Anne for signs of the gardener's boy's tyre dust, a car drew up in the drive instead, out of which stepped no lesser person than the vet himself. Come, or so it seemed from his distraught expression and flapping shirt-sleeves, to beg for urgent help which only my grandmother could give.

The vet's car was followed by the foreman's Land-rover and the studgroom's Moped, and, one after the other, the three drivers were admitted by a stern-faced Alice into the drawing-room. The vet, as befitted his scientific status, was the one to state the reason for their call. There was a grave problem on hand. The confinement of my grandmother's top mare was in progress; the birth was going ahead normally as regards expulsion, but tests had revealed that the foal was a 'blue' foal, its blood group i.e. was incompatible with that of its mother. This meant various unwelcome things: bottle-rearing, fostering, advertising for a substitute mare, the usual palaver, but above all it meant that *on no account* (the implications of the Rhesus factor were of recent knowledge in the stockbreeding world and the vet gave great solemnity to his words, spacing them out and repeating them even more loudly), ON NO ACCOUNT must the newborn animal be allowed to take nourishment from its mother's body. The mare could cleanse the foal, bed down with it, look after it until a foster-mother was found – in fact the longer the two animals stayed together the better, one knew what dangers a motherless foal was exposed to – but she must, somehow, he didn't know how but somehow, be prevented from suckling it.

My grandmother was silent for a while after the vet had spoken. The drawing-room with the three men in it, untidy, heftily shod, faintly smelly, seemed suddenly very small. The foreman and studgroom exchanged glances behind the vet's back – shrewd Suffolk glances implying Rhesus? Jesus! Stuff and nonsense! – and I could tell they reckoned the visit an embarrassment and a waste of time: in their hearts they had already buried the foal and pegged out its skin for slipper linings.

When at last my grandmother spoke, however, the calm, confident tone of her voice seemed to impress even them. 'Mr Knight,' she said, addressing herself solely to the vet, but giving my hand a little squeeze to show me that her words were intended for me as well. 'Dear Mr Knight, I think there is a very simple solution to our problem. Clearly what is needed is a special kind of nosebag which can be clamped over the foal's muzzle the moment it is born. Do you not agree with me? Made of some soft but resilient material through which the mare's milk, even should she try to suckle the foal, cannot pass.'

The vet blinked. My grandmother's suggestion was indeed so simple and homespun I was almost ashamed to hear her make it, but I could see that Mr Knight thought differently. His face lit up, pleased, almost enthusiastic, and only clouded over again after the studgroom and foreman had exchanged a few more shafts of sober Suffolk scepticism. Swapped openly this time, in words, or something akin to them.

'Caan't be worked. Aaan't got no nosebags like 'in.'

'Naa. Nun like 'in.'

'Nun tight enough.'

'Nun small enough.'

'Nun right, nun right for job. Couldn't find 'in, not even down at Erberts'.' (Herberts' was the local saddlers.)

'Couldn't *make* 'in not even down at Erberts'.'

'Naa, naa, naa.' The voices interwove in an impenetrable barrier of counterpoint, thickened by tutting. 'S'right. Ttt, ttt, ttt. Naa, naa, naa. Can't work it, not in a week o' Sundays.'

So implacable was the denial it seemed another stratagem would have to be found that did not involve the unfeasible nosebag, but my grandmother cut through the barrier effortlessly, employing her sweetest and lowest register. I can remember how proud of her I felt at that moment. 'Nonsense,' she said. 'There is no difficulty in the matter at all. The nosebag will be made by us, by my granddaughter and myself. We will make it out of chamois-leather – there should be some in the tack-room, I know some was got in recently because I paid a large bill for it only the other day – and we will fashion and stitch it ourselves, should it take us all night. When is the foal likely to be dropped?'

The vet, after a brief consultation with the stud-groom, said he thought we were still safe for a couple of hours, perhaps three.

'Excellent,' said my grandmother, staring out loftily above the three men's heads so as to bypass any further resistance, 'then someone please go and fetch the material at once. We will start our sewing straight away, there is no time to be lost.'

I remember the night that followed as one of the most thrilling of my life. The drawing-room, from the insignificant outpost it had been until then, was suddenly transformed into a vibrant centre of operations, the headquarters from which a terrible battle – against time, against nature's caprices, against death itself – was to be planned and fought. By us, what was more, by us two expendable females. My grandmother, Sobranies forgotten, wielding her thimble and scissors with the panache of a priestess, began work on the limp piece of chamois-leather on which our fortunes now depended. And I, her chosen acolyte, knelt by her, trying to make myself useful in every way I knew how. I threaded needles for her – her eyesight was no longer sharp enough for threading; I trimmed, I snipped, I checked and double-checked measurements. I liaised with the gardener's boy, shuttling messages back and forth: 'Uterus dilating slowly.' 'Aperture seven inches.' 'Stitching proceeding regularly.' 'Muzzle section completed, only straps to go.' I liaised with the kitchen, fetching cups of reviving consommé (the closest my grandmother would come to Bovril) and taking them back almost untouched. And all the time I glowed inside with a sense of dignity and importance, none the less strong for being vicarious. This, I felt, was a bit more like it. This at last was an occupation worthy of our talents. True, my grandmother and I were not delivering the foal ourselves – that was still the vet's task, the male's prerogative – but this time it was we who were responsible for the outcome. Women, yes, confined to women's quarters and doing women's work, but now, despite the obliqueness of our position, 'in charge' at last in all important senses: ours the idea, ours the implementation, ours the nimble fingers that made such implementation possible. (For even if he had the wits to think it up, I said to myself as I threaded yet more needles – six in a row, with short threads, ready knotted so as to save time – what man could make a contraption such as we were making, so neat, so sturdy, so perfectly fitted to the purpose it was intended to serve?) Ours the merit, therefore, and ours the laurels too. Good, good, good.

The foal's birth took longer than predicted, and finally, despite my protest that I wouldn't move an inch until I knew the animal was alive and well and safely inserted into its nosebag, my grandmother ordered me off to bed. It was well after midnight and I was too tired to argue further, so reluctantly I went.

Next morning I slept late, and my grandmother was already out of the house when I went down for breakfast. I enquired anxiously about the new foal, but nobody, not even Alice who was sister-in-law to the studgroom and served him his early-morning tea, seemed to know how it was or what had happened to it. Perhaps already sensing in this absence of news bad news and not wanting to learn it, I spent the morning reading inside the house, and did not go round to the yard where the foaling-stable was situated until nearly midday.

When I approached the stable I saw immediately that its door was unlatched and unbolted, signifying either that there was someone inside it attending to the mare and foal or else that it was empty. Totally empty, I mean. From the sitting-up room next door I heard the sound of voices, so, skirting the stable without looking into it, I made my way there instead.

Inside I found the studgroom sitting beside a smoking fire, talking to two of the stable hands. When he saw me he quickly dropped a sack he had been holding, letting it fall over a pile of wadding which he seemed to have been in the process of burning, but not before I had noticed the bloodstains.

It was all I needed at this point by way of information. 'It didn't live, then, the foal,' I said, trying to keep my tone as dry and casual as I could: disappointments, as my grandmother had taught me, called for fortitude, especially in front of the staff.

The studgroom shook his head and clicked his tongue inside it philosophically. 'Tch. Didn't live, no, poor little mite.'

There was a silence while he readjusted the sack with his boot and gave a stir to the fire.

'Why not?' I asked. 'What happened? What went wrong? Did it drink its mother's milk after all and get poisoned by it? And if it did, then what about the nosebag? Didn't you get it on in time? Didn't it fit? Didn't it work?'

My questions, in the harsh, Dettol-smelling setting with its laden grate and heap of bloodsoaked tampons, had an almost frivolous ring to them. Perhaps it was my child's high-pitched voice, or perhaps my schoolroom accent, I am not sure, but even to myself I sounded foolish: warbly and faintly out of touch, like the Queen on the wireless.

The studgroom looked at me, then at his colleagues, and let out a laugh. Not a very mirthful one, because his face was drawn and grey and you could see the night's work had made him very tired. 'Tcha!' he said. 'That there nosebag! There's a good one and no mistake! Not much use putting a nosebag on a foal that's already dead.'

There were several other questions I wanted to ask – about the mare and how she was, and whether she was fretting for her lost foal, and whether she would be able to have another next year or if it too would be born 'blue' and dead – but the tone of the studgroom's laughter, in which both the other men now joined, tilting their heads back and wheezing in what seemed to me a very seditious way, warned me that perhaps I had best keep them to myself. There were things – slightly different things – I wanted to ask my grandmother too, but again, when I saw her face at lunchtime, greyer and tireder than the studgroom's even, I decided to leave them unvoiced.

A week or so later, anyway, I was granted an answer to the more far-reaching of my doubts and queries. Not a very articulate one, but a very full and explicit one all the same. Quite by chance, as I was prowling round the kitchen area one afternoon in search of biscuits, I came across Alice sitting in the pantry, brushes and polish ranged before her on the table, wearing the precious nosebag on her hand as if it were a mitt and buffing the silver with it, pliff, pliff, pliff. Humming happily to herself as she buffed, because it was a point of pride in my grandmother's household that nothing in it ever went wasted. This scene told me all I needed to know about the importance of my grandmother's and my great invention, and many other things besides.

After that I took less interest in the destinies of the mares and their foals, and made no more rash assumptions about power and the female line of descent. It upset my grandmother when I told her, but I also gave up embroidery for good.

5

Peachy

My father was generous to me with most things that were his to give, but not with his time. Apart from the bills accruing from it, which he paid smoothly and promptly no matter what their size, my life built up around him unattended to, like a pile of unfolded newspapers of which he barely scanned the headlines – and even this with negative intent, just to make sure that some disaster hadn't struck since the last scanning. The names of my friends, even their number were unknown to him; my progress or regress at school he sanguinely ignored; and as for what I did with my days during the holidays, I doubt the question ever crossed his mind. Save for this unlucky once. I seemed cheerful enough, didn't I, at mealtimes? Healthy? Not pining? Good appetite? Off with me, then, till supper, when he would make another quick routine check.

Because of his otherwise generous nature, however, this skimping with time must have weighed on his conscience, and every now and then – say, once every two years, sometimes three – he would devote an entire afternoon to me: tackling the backlog of my unread school reports with the bored determination of a state-fee'd lawyer, or engaging me in jerky conversation about my future – as cloudy a concept to me as it was to him – or else nailing me in a chair as he tried to teach me the 'Vienna Coup' in bridge, or some other useful female accomplishment.

It was, I think, in this remorseful but well-meaning spirit that one thundery summer's evening, when I was rising ten and passing one of the happiest and most satisfying periods of my life, he came to visit me in my playroom. Or the room I had appointed as my playroom. Or the shed I had adopted for this purpose.

I must try for a moment to see things through his eyes, feel them as he must have felt them. To me, you see, the boiler-shed was without fault, and had been so from the moment I discovered it and claimed it for my own. I loved its warmth, its semi-darkness, its seclusion, and the way noises from the house filtered into it softly, leaving their meanings on the threshold. I loved the high, dust-caked window through which no outsider could spy on what was going on inside. I loved the smell of the place, the cobwebs, the luxurious stuffiness and dryness – so rare in the part and time of England in which we lived. And above all I loved the clutter, and the way it seemed to reflect and confirm to me the history of the house as I knew it: the cans of stiffening paint in long-forgotten colours, the rows of cast-off bicycles belonging to people you could no longer picture ever having ridden one; the trappings of abandoned hobbies – worm-eaten polo mallets, twisted golf-clubs, rusting croquet-hoops, my dead grandfather's ice-skates, my grandmother's badminton racket with her name on it (so it was true, they too had once known how to have fun); all the machines, kits, gadgets and so forth, once vitally required for some purpose or other and now set aside like pensioners to rest. Just to linger in the midst of these things was to me happiness of a very deep and reassuring kind.

Better than lingering, however, I had taken up more or less permanent abode in the shed, at least as regards the day-time. On an already near perfect structure I had engrafted one or two accessories of my own: namely, a tailless, eyeless and horrendously battered old rocking-horse known as Peachy, a shoebox converted to a stable, containing a leaden horse of much, much smaller dimensions, an ochre-coloured stableman's overall, and an antique Chinese wedding headdress complete with bells. With these few additions the furnishing of my micro-paradise was complete. Sustained pleasure is a hard thing to achieve, even for a child, but somehow in this case I had managed it: instinctively or knowingly – I'm not sure which – I had sidestepped all the hedonistic pitfalls and punctured the paradoxes with the worldly wisdom of a Casanova or Don Giovanni. In my cosmos

I had work to do, I had commitment, challenge, leisure, dream-time and rapture, all in sagely dosed proportions: pumice for the puritan in me, syrup for the sybarite.

On the pumice side, for instance, there was the engrossing and potentially endless task of Peachy's repair, which seemed to need re-doing every time I rode him: spare teddy bear's eyes to be cemented into his crumbling sockets with putty, cracks to be stuccoed, wood-worm to be fought, paint to be scraped out of the more tractable of the cans and applied to his chassis (perhaps it is significant that this was how I thought of his body: as a chassis), his rocking mechanism to de-rust, his harness to smarten up and gradually replace – just to name the more pressing of his numerous requirements. Then, still pumice although of a finer grain, there was the germane problem of the shoebox and how to get it to resemble as closely as possible a real stable, in order that Peachy's miniature stand-in (for this was the function of the little leaden horse) could live a convincing equine life when off duty. And in the line of syrup, when I was not acting as architect or carpenter, there were the two divergent roles of stable-lad and Oriental princess to be filled. At pleasure, according to my mood, I could shuffle round my steed, straw in mouth and bucket in hand, grooming, vetting, picking hooves or combating an urgent bout of the strangles, or I could leap into the saddle in regal attire (figuratively leap: in actual fact I had to be very careful about mounting because the saddle was one of the things I hadn't got round to tackling yet and its leather was·badly worn) and gallop off into blue-hazed prairies, with Tartars thundering behind me and wolves snarling at my heels. It was, as you see, as perfect a state of affairs as can be imagined.

But as can *only* be imagined. To my father, coming upon me on one of my more critical stable-hand days, with no imagination to guide him, and guilt doubtless sitting on him like a pair of sunglasses, tinging things even darker than they were, the picture must have seemed very far from ideal. The late hour would not have helped either. Nor the oncoming storm. Nor the overall, which was ragged and swamped me. Nor the fact that Peachy-major was badly lame at the time and rugged-up in a grimy potato sack, and I was kneeling on the ground to massage his fetlocks, crooning to him to keep him quiet, and had been holding this taxing position for the best part of an hour.

Whatever his feelings, however, in finding his only daughter at play in such apparently deprived conditions, my father said nothing. (Otherwise I might have been able to explain, and the misunderstanding might never have arisen.) He merely stalked into the shed, almost wrenching the door from its hinges, and, scooping me from the floor as if I were a dog about to be run over, drew me to him with a bizarre kind of choking sound and pressed my head against his chest, where he held it for what seemed to me ages.

I feared some ugly mishap: the last time my father had acted like this, with such a show of unwarranted emotion, had been the day my grandfather had died.

(That is, the day news had *reached* us that my grandfather had died, which in fact he had done two months earlier, on the other side of the globe, giving everyone ample time to get used to being without him, or so you would have thought.) But when he released me he was smiling and his eyes shone with a light I took to be benevolent but have since learned to recognize as dangerous – wherever and whenever I see it. 'You love horses, Zo-zo darling, don't you?' he said softly. 'You really love them.'

I said politely that I did, up to a certain point, and began to explain to him the peculiar nature of the bond which existed between myself and Peachy. But I doubt my father was paying much attention. His next words, in fact, even more so than the preceding, which had already had a faraway ring to them, seemed to be directed entirely inwards, towards himself.

'Good, good, good,' he muttered. 'Splendid. That settles it then. Horses be it. That is what we'll do.'

Two days later he summoned me to his study. His eyes once again held that perilous philanthropic shine, but I think I knew, even before I saw it, what it was that he had done. It was obvious really, it was what any generous-hearted parent would have done in his place, having the means: he had gone and bought me a real horse, so that I would no longer have to crouch alone in the darkness over the miserable remnants of a wooden one.

My gratitude was enormous, my joy without bounds. And, mysteriously, I suppose, from my father's point of view, even when the real horse was sold again – as it was only a few weeks later, when it was clear that my interest in it had dwindled from zero to below – I went on thanking him, time after time, for his gift. I just couldn't help it.

To my father, this attitude of mine merely added injury to the initial insult of my refusal. 'I don't see what point there is in your thanking me, Zoë,' he would say thinly, looking away from me as if the mere sight of me offended him: he must have known I had taken to the boiler-shed again because I was hardly ever out of the place now so busy was I, but the fact no longer seemed to trouble him, indeed I think my perverseness in this matter afforded him a bitter kind of satisfaction. 'You didn't seem to appreciate my gift one bit. I'm told you even maimed the wretched animal, or disfigured it in some way. Certainly I know I got far less for it than I gave when it came to re-selling. So either you are insincere, or else your concept of appreciation must be very different from mine.'

I suppose my concepts, many of them, not just the one in question, *were* different from my father's. And I suppose this difference was what lay at the root of our present misunderstanding – and of all the countless misunderstandings that followed, because, sad but true, this apparently insignificant business of the gift-horse marked the first, spidery crack of a rift that was to divide us for life. I suppose this rather than its converse, knowing that in the haystack of personal relationships it is idle to seek for single needles of cause – especially rusty old ones whose points are blunt.

And yet I sometimes wonder. Had my father ignored what he perceived as this terrible slight against him; had he, just for one brief moment, suspended judgement, taken my gratitude as genuine and come back to the shed to see me at play – or rather at work – combing and plaiting the resplendent new mane and tail that, thanks to his generosity and my ingenuity, now sprouted with every appearance of authentic growth from the neck and rump of my beloved Peachy, then – or so, at any rate, I sometimes tell myself – perhaps he would have understood, and there would have been no crack, no rift, no estrangement between us ever.

On the other hand, I sometimes tell myself, or, more correctly, am told by other people, that if my father *had* observed me thus occupied, our estrangement would have been total and immediate; he would have found my hijacking of the horsehair so incomprehensible, they say, he would have thought he had begotten a Martian. So there, and maybe things were better the way they were.

6

Ferdinand and Isabella

Father Raymond Daubeny – or d'Aubeny as it was written on the school notice-board where the timetable of his visit was set out in all its luscious, mouth-watering detail – was the first true star I had ever seen.

That any of us had ever seen, and that went for the nuns as well. Only I suppose he was more like a comet than a star really, in that his appearances were periodic and fairly predictable, and that all that we middle-school students could actually count on seeing of him was the dust of his long majestic tail as he swept across our small segment of sky.

He came to the Convent once every six years – when he was not teaching in America or suffering from a mysterious and romantic-sounding complaint of the spinal cord which afflicted him from time to time, in which case the interval might be even longer – expressly to talk to newcomers, school-leavers and those undergoing any particularly knotty spiritual difficulties. Thus your chances of meeting him face to face alone and actually being spoken to by him were roughly those of being killed at Russian roulette, or so I worked out. (And your chances of speaking back were even slighter, because it was well known that his presence robbed even the suavest sixth-formers of their words. On his last visit, the then head of the school had only managed to utter her name, and that was all. The exchange was lore by now: 'And who are you?' Father Raymond had allegedly asked. 'Elizona,' the girl had replied. 'Elizona?' he had said smiling. 'What sort of a name is that? Sounds like stuff you put down the lavatory to clean it.' After which intoxicating touch of intimacy, further conversation on the poor girl's part had naturally become impossible.) For the hundreds of less fortunate pupils whose birthdates did not coincide with the orbit, contact was limited to hearing him say mass in the morning and benediction in the evening, to sitting through his lectures if you could manage it, to catching tantalizing glimpses of him disappearing down corridors or striding along the breviary-walk deep in meditation, and to leaving your copy of his prayer-book in a pile outside his room for him to autograph when he had time. A congruous donation to his pet charity and you could even obtain a signed photograph, but the photographs were all the same and there was little prestige in possessing one.

I was thirteen, not a newcomer, not a school-leaver, not prey to convincing spiritual tangles – although I admit that the idea of cooking one up rapidly in order to gain a hearing did occur to me, only sadly I just couldn't think of anything suitable in time. So while my theoretical chances of obtaining the longed-for goal of a private audience might have been one in six, my actual chances were zero. I would not obtain one now, nor later, nor indeed ever; it was a simple matter of dates and bad luck. I had some difficulty believing in my misfortune, accustomed as I was to coming first in things and standing out in the crowd and generally getting my own way, but in this case I simply had to acknowledge that Fate had cast me on to the slagheap. If I could get past the barrier and be admitted into the august presence – just for one minute get the beam of Father Raymond's magnificent ascetic's eye to light on me and see me as a distinct person under the drab school uniform and regulation pinafore – then I knew that I would somehow manage to make the eye rest there and marvel at what it saw. I had few doubts about my powers of seduction once they were unleashed. But I could not cross the barrier, and there was an end to it.

I chafed under my impotence for days. No, worse, I burned, I frizzled. Scorning half-measures I refused to do as other attention-seekers did, jostling themselves into the front benches in church, hanging around outside afterwards, laughing immoderately at Father Raymond's jokes during lectures, or sticking their tongues out to abnormal length while taking communion from his hands. These seemed to me self-defeating devices: better to make no mark at all than to be remembered for your tonsils or your giggle. Even when one of the younger nuns explained to us a very ticklish question about Matter and Form and the Soul which had been bothering her and asked which of us would like to put it to Father Raymond in her place at the end of his next lecture, I did not volunteer. It wasn't that I didn't like the question – I thought it sounded very profound and philosophical and could quite fancy myself standing up to ask it – it was that I still wanted somehow, if I was to emerge at all, to emerge in my own right, as a result of my own propulsion.

My instinct was sound in this case as it turned out. When the question was asked it came out very parroty and stilted, and Father Raymond, instead of dwelling on the unlucky mouthpiece, cast his eyes knowingly towards the back rows where the nuns were seated and scrutinized them one by one, smiling, and saying something spicy-sounding in Latin. When he reached Sister Martha, whose question it was, she went the colour of a Kit-Kat wrapper, poor woman, and he smiled all the more. So, no, I was glad I hadn't burnt my chances on that one.

Particularly since towards the end of the lecture another chance cropped up, a highly promising one this time, and one that I did not lose a second in snatching. Quite in what connection I don't remember, but Father Raymond had got on to snakes – something,

I imagined, to do with devils, although to tell the truth he seemed to be defending them more than otherwise so perhaps I imagined wrong. 'Nobody really likes these poor creatures,' he was saying whimsically, 'and yet when you get to know them they are such *de*lightful animals. Not slimy as you might think, not base, not treacherous, not aggressive, but clean and cuddly and friendly. The non-poisonous varieties in fact make . . . ' and he shelled the words out staccato for better effect ' . . . simply . . . wonderful . . . pets'. Then he paused for a moment to accommodate the inevitable squeals and murmurs of surprise, before going on to enquire rhetorically, 'Does anybody here believe me, though? Is there anybody willing to put it to the test?'

He was just about to add a routine, No, of course not, or words to that effect, prior to rounding off his lecture altogether, when my voice rang out. A little louder than I had intended, perhaps, but the *force de frappe* was important. 'I do, Father! I love snakes, I think they're fantastic! I'd love nothing better than to keep one as a pet.'

The coveted gaze swung towards me like a spotlight and for a brief moment was mine. I stood up and held it, glaring like an owl: intensity was my only weapon and I hurled it hard. I suspected that even Lucrezia Borgia would have been hard put to cull her victim in such circumstances, cloaked in this abominable school attire and with her hair cropped like coconut matting, but my trust in myself was high and I refused to contemplate the possibility of a miss.

I would dazzle, enslave, and conquer on the spot or I would burst.

There followed a brief and rather uneasy silence as my target and I confronted one another. Stars do not necessarily take kindly to a sudden change of script, and it struck me that the opening I had chosen might not be as clever as I had thought. Then mercifully, before things got too uncomfortable, from the back Sister Martha intervened in her chirpy voice to break the tension, introducing me and explaining laughingly not to worry, that Zoë always took the opposite view of everything.

'And quite right too,' said Father Raymond, echoing the nun's laughter and recovering his charm so quickly that it seemed he had never lost it. 'The dialectic principle in action. Thesis and Antithesis.' And he added something else in a foreign language – not Latin this time but a language I didn't recognize.

Whether Sister Martha recognized it either, or indeed anyone else present in the room, I greatly doubt, but there was the usual burst of sycophantic laughter, and on this note the lecture came to its end.

Not so, however, my acquaintance with Father Raymond. In line with the steepest and most ambitious of my predictions, we were indeed only at the beginning. He summoned us to his study – myself and Sister Martha – that very evening, in the interval between benediction and supper, where he received us crouched behind an enormous desk, grinning like a tarantula in a party mood. Did I really mean what I had said earlier in the lecture-hall, he wanted to know? If so, he had thought up a very interesting and amusing idea that he would like to put to me. Would my parents agree to the expense of five pounds or so for a ventilated glass box the size of a small aquarium? It shouldn't cost more than that, he didn't think. They would? Splendid, then *he* would provide the snakes. A pair of them (a quick look here at Sister Martha, no doubt to sound out the official Convent attitude to this daring scheme) because together they would be less lonely. Grass snakes he thought would be best – at any rate to start with. Then, if the experiment was successful, we could pass to bigger fry: pythons, boas, perhaps even anacondas if they didn't thrash around too much and need too much water. As luck would have it he was spending all this year and part of the next in a monastery near by, working on his . . . er . . . *magnum opus*, dare he call it, (another quick glance at Sister Martha here: the *opus* and its composition was a topic of almost sacred importance among the nuns) and could pop in now and again to keep an eye on things and see how they were going. What did I have to say to this plan? Did it strike me as a good one?

For a moment, like the mythical Elizona, I was speechless. True, I had laboured for just this result; true, I had repeated my owl stint during benediction, staring into Father Raymond's eyes when he turned to present the Sacrament until what with the emotion and the brightness of the gold monstrance I had gone almost dizzy. But even so I couldn't help feeling that the result was in some way disproportionate to the effort involved. The granting of an interview I would have understood. (Preferably on my own, though, without Sister Martha whose presence I found superfluous and faintly irritating at this stage.) Followed by a second interview, leading to a third and so forth, in gradual or even rapid progression. But an immediate proposal of joint-ownership of a pair of snakes – which *he*, mark you, he, the elusive and glamorous Father d'Aubeny, who only visited the Convent once every six years, would 'pop in to see now and again' as if he were a relative or a vet – this seemed to me almost bewilderingly much.

A true seductress, however, does not remain bewildered for long by the size and speed of her successes, and I soon adjusted myself to the facts. Quicker than I had bargained for, perhaps, but the compelling owl-stare technique had evidently worked: this star, this comet, this bright and unattainable object of desire had come to rest at my Daniel Neal-clad feet and was waiting humbly for me to pick it up. Under such circumstances, and with Sister Martha at my elbow, pink-faced with excitement, nudging me to accept, what else could I do but oblige?

I entered into the project as I imagine a saint enters heaven: bowled over by happiness but with an underlying sense of sound personal achievement. I obtained the money – Father Raymond's name was a byword in chic Catholic circles and my parents were almost as flattered as I was at the idea of our venture; I obtained the glass container. I filled it with earth and stones and plants. I bought two special saucers, one for milk and one for water. I bought packets of dehydrated fish-food which I thought would probably do quite well for a start – these were early days to catch live flies or whatever it was that grass snakes fed on. And then I sat back to await the arrival of the container's inhabitants. Ah, yes, and with an eye to further immeshing Father Raymond in my snares by my originality I chose their names: Ferdinand and Isabella.

Sister Martha had taken to flanking me regularly during this phase of preparation, and it became tacitly understood that she would be present during all the priest's future visits. This did not bother me much any more, I assumed she had been placed there by her superiors for propriety's sake, rather like a duenna or a gynaecologist's nurse. And when I remembered the uncomfortable burning quality of Father Raymond's gaunt-set eyes on the two momentous occasions when they had locked with mine, I could well understand why. Indeed it gave me almost a sense of safety to know that I would not be alone with my apparently docile but still very unpredictable admirer.

I was doubly glad of the nun's presence when the snakes finally arrived, because they revolted me instantly. It was all I could do to transfer them from their travelling box to their container without retching. Had it not been for Sister Martha, who seemed to guess my horror and stood by me encouragingly, holding the

lid poised over the case ready to slap it into place and
stop the snakes escaping, I don't think I would have
managed even this first simple operation. Uncaring of
my Borgia image, I would have lurched out of the
room and made straight for the nearest basin.

Somehow, though, with Sister Martha's support, I
managed to overcome my disgust. And with Father
Raymond's eyes on me, already narrowing a little in
amused speculation, I cast my face into a delighted
mask, took the box from him with genuinely confused
thanks, and with a shriek that I hoped would pass for
one of joy, opened it over the glass case and shook
the contents unceremoniously downward. Uggggh.
Grabbing hard at Sister Martha's sleeve on the way
to make sure she didn't miss her cue and muff the
closure.

With the lid firmly in place I felt stronger, and was
able to narrow my own eyes back at Father Raymond
and shine according to programme. I enthused over the
beauty of the two repugnant creatures he had brought
me, told him the names I had chosen ('Then this is
no glass box, Zoë, but the Escorial.' 'Precisely, Father,
the Escorial, and if they lay eggs we will call them
Infantas.' Ping-pong of witticisms, better even than I
had imagined.) And more in this dashing, gratifying
vein. Towards the end of the interview I was even
able to push back the lid of the case a hand's breadth
and touch one of the snakes on the flank, casting
another sideways look at Father Raymond as I did
so. He looked back lingeringly, smilingly, and I could

tell that the gesture had amused him. Things seemed
to be going exactly as they should.

'Would you not take one of them and wind it round
your neck, Zoë? That would look very pretty. No?
Well, perhaps you are right, we must allow them to
get settled in first. Then later on, maybe. There are all
sorts of tricks that it will be fun to try, later on.' And he
smiled again, this time in the direction of Sister Martha,
who looked away.

They say that the secret of power is to relinquish it
before it has been taken from you. Whether or not I
was unconsciously following this maxim when I made
my decision I do not know, but I certainly felt a great
sense of rightness when I carried it out. What I did was
this. Immediately after I had left the visitors' parlour
with my prize (and thus at the crowning moment of
my success, when I had my scaly trophies to display
to everyone and a two-sided conversation with Father
Raymond to report of such length and brilliance that it
would make school history for years), instead of going
to wow my public as I had planned, I slipped out of a
side-door, container in arms and head well averted, and
made straight for the lake at the bottom of the garden,
where I overturned the entire caboosh into the water
and then set about breaking the glass walls to fragments
with a stone.

My version of the facts, for Sister Martha and the
others, was that while seeking special pondy titbits
for Ferdinand and Isabella I had tripped and fallen.

How sad, everyone would say, how embarrassing, what rotten, rotten luck.

To Sister Martha, as to myself, the incident seemed to come as a relief. She said she would ask Reverend Mother to explain to Father Raymond what had happened, she was sure he would understand. She made no mention of our replacing the lost animals ourselves or continuing the experiment, in fact from that day forward she spoke to me very seldom, and never about snakes.

This was not quite the end of the matter as far as I was concerned, though. I never saw Father Raymond again, nor did I write to him, but after the riddance of Ferdinand and Isabella, for several nights running, and thenceforward at intervals for years, I had a dream in which he played a significant part. In times of stress I have it even now. It goes like this. I am standing by the lake, the container smashed and empty beside me, looking into the waters with a sense of liberation, when suddenly I see the snakes swimming purposefully towards me. They look very vindictive, their heads are reared, their mouths are open, their scales are puffed wide with hatred; I can smell them giving off a kind of venomous fart from the entire length of their bodies as they advance. They pause by the broken cage, turning over the fragments as if anxious to build it up again and return to it. Then, seeing the impossibility of this, they continue their pursuit. I run, as one runs in dreams, lead-footed and hardly moving, with the knowledge that they are behind me and gaining ground. Suddenly, from nowhere, Father Raymond appears. A friendly, helpful Father Raymond, nothing of the vamp about him at all. 'Why are you running, Zoë?' he asks. 'To get away from *them*, Father,' I reply, indicating the snakes which by now are almost on me. 'Ttt, ttt, ttt,' he says, shaking his head. 'Useless. Snakes can run faster than you, they can swim faster, using the turbo principle they can also fly. Your only hope is to stand still and pretend you are a tree. If you do, there is one chance in six that they will fall for it and entwine themselves round your neck as if it were the trunk and go to sleep there. Then you can deal with them later. That, anyway, is my advice.' And he disappears. And I stand still, waiting: a terrified, bogus tree with the odds stacked against me.

7

Bernard

My first in any way successful encounter with romantic love took place in the town of Blois in France (or perhaps it is a city, I am afraid my attention that day was not for cathedrals) when I was fifteen.

I was on holiday, visiting the castles of the Loire valley in the company of a schoolfriend and her parents, and Blois was the third stop on our schedule. We did not make an overnight stay – Mrs Braithwaite, my friend's mother, was avid for 'atmosphere' and had read in her guidebook that the place was blessed by a large chocolate factory – but we made a longish halt, punctuated by lunch. And after lunch, as the wine took its effect on the two elder Braithwaites and they stretched out in their chairs, releasing Gauloise fumes into an already charged sky, my friend and I – 'les girls' as Colonel Braithwaite had taken to calling us from the moment we crossed the channel – were allowed to roam about on our own. We were given an hour, and were told to keep to the main streets and to meet up back at the restaurant when the time was up.

Provincial towns, even cities, even French cities, were reputedly quiet, safe places in those days. Even so, I imagine that the Braithwaite parents imagined that their daughter and I would do our roaming together. But since the condition was not made explicit, and since the seams of our school-based friendship were already under strain, the moment we were out of sight of the restaurant my friend and I split up in tacit accord and went our different ways.

Having no talent for path-finding, indeed a great talent for path-losing, I decided I had better play safe and choose one road and stick to it, following wherever it lead for half an hour and then doubling back again. This I duly did, and after about ten minutes' leisurely walking I found myself already in a drabber, more industrial area; by the smell of it, and by the increasing number of hoardings advertising its product, in the neighbourhood of the dreaded chocolate factory. Town or city as it may have been, at that time Blois was definitely small. I was just about to turn round and pursue my walk in the opposite direction, in the hope that the other segment of the road would have more to offer than high brick walls and warehouses and giant images of mud-brown chocolate, when a lorry drew up beside me and a young man descended from the cockpit and came straight towards me with a smile.

Like Paul bustling to Damascus with a clear brief and all his thoughts in order, I was smitten, knocked off my course, cast into confusion. And just as suddenly restored to perfect harmony. The young man came to within a foot of me, then stopped and opened his arms wide, and I, as if mesmerized, stepped into them and allowed them to close about me. Plaf! and I had found my haven.

Smut at school was rife, and I probably knew more about the theoretical side of sex than any other subject — which, as will emerge later on in another story, was not saying very much. Nothing of what I had learnt, however, none of the notions I had so laboriously collected and trimmed and cobbled together to form the uneven patchwork of my knowledge, seemed to have any bearing on the dynamics of the present encounter. Sex, as I had been taught to recognize it, fear it and sneer at it, simply did not come into the picture. The young lorry-driver and I did not eye one another, or flare our nostrils, or cast smouldering looks the way adults did in films — apart from anything else we had not the time before we joined. Nor did we kiss or grope or fumble with one another's clothing in the approved (or disapproved) manner, the way people of our own age-group did at parties. There was no snogging between us, no smooching or petting or necking or whatever it was called in those days. We simply clung to one another in an ecstatic kind of peace, fitting together appropriately like the sundered halves of a vase or flowerpot that have been rejoined.

Later – I don't know how much later, but I presume the embrace, timeless as it seemed, couldn't have lasted more than two and half to three minutes – we separated slightly and looked at one another in amazement. Amazement that we should have met. Amazement that we should have recognized one another. Or perhaps amazement that, things between us standing as they did, we should not have met before. On my side there was also the bonus amazement of looking into the kindest, sweetest and most beautiful face, male or female, live or pictured, that I had ever seen or could ever imagine seeing. Alain Delon in his heyday with Saint Francis of Assisi inside him looking out, to give the idea. With a touch of Richard Burton, too – the explorer, not the actor – about the eyebrows and cheekbones.

'Bernard,' said this peerless amalgam of male qualities when at last he spoke, pointing to his chest. It seemed natural at that point that he should know a priori I was foreign. 'Et toi?'

'Zoë.'

'Zoë.' He nodded, as if my name too were a well-known piece of information, temporarily mislaid and now come back to him, and tilting back my head with his finger, he placed a kiss on each of my eyes in turn as he repeated the vowels separately. 'Zo . . . ë.' Then, like a stag or a jackal he threw back his own head and made a funny kind of noise, half bray, half whoop. An acknowledgement to the heavens, I think it was, a thank-you to the Fates for uniting us. It did not surprise me; it was what I felt like doing myself. 'Zoë, ma Zoë, enfin. Bien arrivée.' Welcome.

This was our meeting, our greeting to one another. How the rest of our time together was spent I scarcely remember, save that we laughed a lot because we were so happy, and cross-talked a lot too because of the urgency of squeezing certain vital messages through the holes in the language-barrier. (Nor, for that matter, do I really know how long we *were* together. Mrs Braithwaite, packing me in the car again with trembling hands, said they had been looking for me for three whole hours, but surely this was an exaggeration. I should think an hour and three-quarters is closer to the mark.) Perhaps we sat in the café and had something to drink, perhaps we didn't. Perhaps we met a friend of Bernard's with a dog, since I have a faint memory of exchanging words of love with him across the pelt of a Breton spaniel; or, again, perhaps not. Mostly I think we just wandered up and down the street (the same street we had met on, within sight of the lorry), hand in hand and soul in soul, until aroused from our dream by the screech of Colonel Braithwaite's tyres breaking alongside, and the sound of his wife's voice, raised in relief and horror mixed.

I betrayed this love, of course I did – quicker and cheaper than Judas. Mrs Braithwaite descended from the car like a Fury, brandishing a stick of freshly bought French bread which was presumably all she had found in the car by way of a weapon, and lunged towards Bernard, jabbering in remarkably effective French that he was to take himself off immediately. 'Shoo! Shoo! Allez-vous en, horrible homme!' she yelled. How dare he, a 'misérable ouvrier', lay his hands on a 'jeune fille de bonne famille' like me. She would call the police, the gendarmes, she would have him thrown in prison if he didn't leave this moment. 'Shoo! Away avec vous! Allez! Disparaître, disparaître! Tout de suite, compris? Lointain!' And seeing the scrap of paper in his hands which I had given him, bearing my home address and telephone number, she tore it from him and stuffed it officiously into her bag before delivering a parting kick to the cuffs of his jeans.

And that was all there was to it really. Bernard did not react: a man with a face like that cannot stoop to discourtesy or haggling. He merely opened his hands and looked at them as if watching whatever they had been holding fall to the ground, and then looked back at me; trusting, I suppose, that I would pick it up.

To my shame, I did nothing. I returned to the car with Mrs Braithwaite and allowed myself to be driven away into the anonymity of the Loir-et-Cher twilight without so much as a wave or a sign. What was more, I immediately, and with craven co-operation, subscribed to that version of events which Mrs Braithwaite seemed to have decided in the meantime that it was more comfortable for all four of us to believe. I was not to be cast as naughty Zoë, I was to be poor Zoë. Somehow we two girls had lost sight of one another – careless of us, but there it was, on that account we were both equally to blame – and I had wandered off on my own and been importuned, harassed, taken advantage of by a louche French wolf on the prowl. My address had been extracted from me, by force or cunning. It had been clever of me to keep calm like that, not to contrast the wretch but to appear to second his designs, but I was to remember that the next time anything like that happened, the best defence was simply to march on with my head in the air and refuse to speak at all. 'That is what nice girls do, Zoë, girls of your background. So mind you do the same in future.' The Colonel, a little belatedly, intervened in support of his wife's efforts. 'That's right, my girl,' he confirmed. 'Keep aloof, chin up, eyes straight ahead, and these tuppenny-ha'penny Latin lover-boys will know that there is nothing doing.'

I nodded sagely to all this. Obscurely, I think I was relieved that someone else's snobbishness had intervened to pre-empt my own. Bernard had described his family to me, the house that he was building with his savings on the outskirts of Blois – conveniently near the road for the parking of the 'camion'. Would I have enjoyed being mistress of such an establishment? Would I even have enjoyed *thinking* that I might enjoy it? I was grateful, I suppose, that I did not have to set myself these questions, let alone answer them. I am afraid to say I even joined in the praise, when, shock subsiding, the conversation shifted to Mrs Braithwaite's linguistic competence and the richness of her vocabulary – two things which seemed to have surprised herself even more than her listeners, with the possible exception of Bernard. 'Was I really?' she twittered delightedly in response to our compliments. 'Do you really think so? I must say, I *did* think it came over rather well. All I could think of saying when I got out of the car was, "Buzzez Offay!", but then it somehow all came back to me. Just shows, it's like they say, like riding a bicycle, you never really lose the knack.' Contentment restored, at least in the Braithwaite camp.

I settled down in the back of the car, chewing listlessly on a piece of the brandished bread filled with chocolate from the chocolate factory (the Colonel's recipe for overcoming the unpleasantness of the afternoon), and inspected the wound in my heart with detachment. I was fifteen, I had explored, so to speak, only a handkerchief of the world's terrain, and already that handkerchief had yielded me a Bernard. To have him torn from me with such promptness was sad, but signified nothing. By the simple laws of probability the planet must be crawling with Bernards: bigger Bernards, better Bernards, Bernards in Blois and Blakeney and Bloemfontein. It was just a question of visiting new places and keeping my eyes and options open. Still chewing, but already with more punch in my molars, I reached for the road-map to see what was the name of our next destination.

It was only later – much, *much* later, when I had learnt more about the laws of probability and their scant relevance to love, or even to friendly sex – that the wound began, very faintly, very gently, to throb. As it does now, and serve me right.

8

The Father Confessor

In my last year at the Convent a change took place in the priest situation. Instead of having to rely on the parish curate for the regular weekly sacraments, and on visiting celebrities like Father d'Aubeny for extra spiritual titbits to be thrown our way, the school took on a resident chaplain. Whether lent or rented, I do not know, but a neighbouring monastery sent us a member of their confraternity to live in the hitherto untenanted 'priest's cottage' behind the church and act as our on-the-spot confessor.

I was one of the fortunate pupils who were allowed to help with the preparations for the chaplain's arrival. From the legal point of view I suppose it was a little bit fly of the nuns to make use of our unpaid labour like this, prospecting it as a favour, but for us it was truly fun. It was sort of Snow White work: opening up the cobwebby windows, dusting the neglected rooms, hanging curtains, carrying in furniture, trying to make things clean and cheerful for the new occupant. Father Crispin had suffered badly in the war, we were told by the nun in charge of the cleaning-up operations, he needed warmth and comfort and plenty of space for his books. So we knocked up extra shelves for him in carpentry class, and made two special woolly foot-mats, one for his sitting-room and one to go beside his bed.

When the new chaplain arrived, those like myself who had done all these things in a motherly, protective spirit were rather disconcerted. The man was huge, and very, very old-looking. He was also clumsy, and remote from worldly matters to the point of rudeness. The Reverend Mother had us all line up in the main room of the cottage to welcome him and receive his thanks for our interior-decorating job, but he scarcely seemed to notice the efforts we had made. With a shoe the size of an ironing-board he lunged into the mat and sent it skidding, rocking the table that was set on it and upsetting the vase of wild flowers we had picked. 'Um,' he said without apology, 'flowers. Or are they weeds? I always wonder where the demarcation line is set,' and proceeded to pick up the fallen flowers one by one and cast them into the fireplace, dripping water everywhere. Then, sensing from our silence that perhaps some more recognizable sign of appreciation was called for, he dropped himself into the fireside armchair from his immense height and let out a kind

of frightened bellow aimed in our direction. 'Errumm!'
he said. 'Yes, well. Errumm! Very nice, I suppose, very
nice. I am fond of flowers. Weeds too.' After which
he stared into the grate, puce-faced and silent, until
Reverend Mother signalled from behind his back that
the welcome ceremony was over and we were to mop
up the mess and file out.

How I first began to become friends with this almost
paranoically shy and reclusive man (because that, I
eventually discovered, was all his off-putting behaviour
was due to: shyness), I do not remember. I can't think I
was particularly drawn to him in any way, my interests
at the time were almost exclusively in spot-clearing
remedies and boyfriends and how to procure both
when I had neither. I can't think he can have felt
drawn to me either: of all the beings he shunned,
hormone-rich females on the brink of womanhood
must have come top of his list. How did we ever
get through to one another, then, I wonder? How did
we first recognize the things that united us across the
quadruple barrier of age and sex and indifference and
fright? I honestly do not recall. All I know is that, as
time went on, and particularly during my last summer
term, when exams were looming, and the days were
longer and we were granted more evening freedom for
study, I found myself, more and more often, ditching
my books and wandering over to the priest's cottage for
a chat with Father Crispin. Usually invited, and usually
carrying with me packets of Mars Bars to share with
my host, who loved them but could not afford them.

Once it had become established, however, the sheer unlikelihood of the friendship enchanted us both. Father Crispin, war-shattered, world-shattered really, I suppose, poor man, seemed at first unable to believe that intellectual company was being afforded him by such an improbable partner, and would keep jerking up his head in mid-discussion and staring at me, as if to say, And what are *you* doing here, young woman, may I ask, getting in the way and upsetting my concentration? But gradually he seemed to accept the contrast and even take pleasure in it. Sometimes, before we settled into our argument for the evening, he would even go so far as to compliment me on some aspect of my appearance; in order to underline, as it were, the fact that he now recognized me as female and forgave me for it. 'Your nose, Zoë, is of a classical mould, did anyone ever tell you?' 'Your hair, child, is nice and abundant but would look better tied.' 'Is that lipstick, may I enquire, that you are wearing? Oh, lipsalve, is it? How interesting, what a pretty shine it gives.'

I, for my part, found reassurance in the contrast. Had I enjoyed this type of speculative conversation with a man who attracted me physically, I would have mistrusted my motives, thought I was only in it for the flattery. But as it was I could relax and enjoy the argument for argument's sake. It was my first taste of pure intellectual sparring, my first awareness, really, that I possessed a brain that was in any way suited to this kind of skirmish, and the discovery delighted me. After each meeting, as I made my way back to the darkened school building in the late summer twilight. I felt skittish and powerful, like a colt that had just realized its jumping potential or a baby tiger that has found its claws.

Anyway, however it first started up, and whatever its basis and the reasons for its equilibrium, the fact remains that both Father Crispin and myself derived great pleasure from our curiously assorted friendship. To begin with, in our discussions we stuck to fairly bland and trouble-free issues. Does everything that has volume have a shape as well? Could a completely new colour be imagined? Could you describe the taste of pineapple to someone who had never eaten one? This sort of limbering-up exercise, very much practice-gloves-on and safety-visors-down. I suppose he was testing my reliability, seeing if I kept our conversations to myself or reported them to the nuns. We would read bits of Berkeley as well, and Plato and More (the one with the one *o*, not the one with two). But as the weeks passed and no complaints reached him, he began to open up his mind and his books to me with ever-growing candour: Locke, Hume, Wittgenstein, the Frankfurt School, the Vienna Circle; sceptics, positivists, pragmatists, all the ists and isms there were; Hegel and Schopenhauer, even passages from Nietzsche and Machiavelli – we went through the lot, arguing and criticizing and blaming and praising and dotting the pages with flakes of chocolate in our excitement.

Nor did we limit ourselves to philosophy. Father Crispin had a small telescope – one of the few possessions he had been allowed to keep, he told me a little wistfully, when he entered the monastery – and on clear nights we would train it on the sky and he would point out the stars to me, telling me their names and sizes and distances from earth, citing figures which rang in my ears like poetry: a billion miles, a trillion particles, three hundred million light years. ('And how many mutton chops placed end on end to reach the moon? One, madam, provided it were long enough.' This was Father Crispin, taking the mickey out of Doctor Johnson, whom he said he considered a terrible old toad.) Oh, yes, we enjoyed ourselves all right, the bashful boffin and his acne-ridden apprentice. In our strange lopsided way we really did have fun together, really did do one another good.

Sadly, though, while what the good Father Crispin did to me endured and in a sense endures to this day, the good I did to him did not. Through whose fault it is difficult to say, but all benefits I brought him, save for the Mars Bars, were rendered null in the space of a few minutes, and in the following tragicomic way. As exam-time drew near and the school year approached its close, those of us like myself who were leaving for more exotic places of education were summoned one afternoon to the Reverend Mother's study – her 'parlour' as it was called in the quaint Convent idiom – for a briefing on certain delicate matters which until now had been considered too advanced for our comprehension. The first point, surprisingly enough, concerned the Virgin Mary. Now that we were going 'out into the world', we were told, we would often hear the Blessed Virgin held up to scorn and covered with the most vile abuse. It happened constantly – at social gatherings, at dinner parties, even in the houses of friends where one would least expect it. (Where and by whom, I often wonder, was this piece of intelligence gathered? And when did it date from? The Reformation? It is the 'constantly' in particular that intrigues me.) Because we were not, alas, living in a Catholic country. Now, the best thing, the cleverest thing, we could do when we found ourselves in such a situation was to rise, say quietly but firmly, 'The lady you are discussing happens to be a friend of mine,' and leave the room. Our popularity would not suffer, quite the opposite: in the end people would admire us for standing up for our beliefs, and we would be asked to more and more parties.

This was the first piece of worldly instruction with which the Reverend Mother saw fit to equip us. The second was slightly more pertinent. Indeed, as far as I was concerned, it was all too pertinent. Now that we were growing up, she went on, transferring her gaze to the stucco-work above our heads and leaving it there for safety's sake until she had finished speaking and for some moments afterwards, we would sometimes find – perhaps some of the more developed among us had *already* found – that there were certain movements, certain activities, like riding a bicycle over cobblestones, for example, or sitting in a bath of very hot water (?), that quite independent of one's will provoked a pleasurable sensation in the nether regions of the body.

Now, we were not to be taken in by this: the sensation might be pleasing, but in the eyes of God it was not. The feeling could come to anyone, at any time, and in itself was harmless, at most a venial sin and a small one. But, attention! To indulge in the feeling, to solicit it, to try to prolong it, turned the venial sin into a grave sin, a *mortal* one, which went under the justly hideous name of Self-Abuse. Would we remember this? We would? Then that, she thought, was all for the time being. On the last day of term she would receive us singly for another little chat before we left. Goodbye, my dears, and close the door quietly, and say nothing of all this to the younger ones. Respect their innocence.

As I left the parlour the floor seemed to buckle under my feet. That was *all*? An incalculable load of mortal sin thrust on my shoulders in the space of a minute, and the woman had the callousness to say that that was all? And what did she mean, innocence of the younger ones? Not if they were like me! No, not if they were like me! I made for the garden to think things over. It was clear, horribly clear, that what had up till now seemed to me a simple technique for warming myself up in bed at night and getting off to sleep came squarely into the category of sinful activities the Reverend Mother had described. Into the category of *mortally* sinful activities, what was more. I was shattered by the revelation. Night after night, year after year (although thankfully not so often in the summer when it was warmer, or at home where the beds were drier), by what had seemed to me the blameless and rather nifty system of pressing

my thighs together and waiting for a sweet kind of
heat-giving explosion to take place, more functional
than any hot-water bottle, I had been committing
heinous, soul-destructive mortal sin. The weight of
guilt was almost more than I could bear.

That evening and every following evening until
the end of the week when confessions were heard,
I avoided going to the priest's cottage: I was sorry
to hurt Father Crispin's feelings, but I was afraid
of dirtying the place by my presence. When at last
at eleven o'clock on Friday morning the bell for
confessions rang, I hurried across to the church and
knelt down in the front pew, anxious to get things over
with as quickly as possible. As I knelt there waiting, I
tried not to think of anything that would interfere with
my resolve: confession is secret, I repeated to myself,
the priest is an instrument. I am not confessing to
my friend Father Crispin, I am confessing to God.
If I keep my sins and go to communion on Sunday
I will be committing another sin, every bit as grave;
if I do *not* go to communion I will be rejecting God
and committing yet another. I must shut my eyes and
go ahead with it, I must, I must, I must.

Despite my determination, when Father Crispin's
ham-sized hand came through the curtain of the confessional and beckoned the first penitent to approach,
I very nearly funked it. Only a stab on the shoulder
from a supervising nun saved me from backing out and
running away unshriven. From that moment onwards,
however, things suddenly became very smooth and easy

to perform. I knelt in the confessional, put my face to the grille (useless to hang back in the shadows or try to disguise my identity, the mesh was notoriously transparent), and blurted out the opening formula. 'Bless me, Father, for I have sinned,' compressing it into a bare three syllables, 'Ble, fa, sind', and leaving out altogether the half a confiteor or whatever it was that one was supposed to mumble to oneself at this stage. Scarcely waiting for the blessing to be delivered I then hurried on to the next bit, 'It is one week since my last confession. These are the sins for which I beg forgiveness . . . ' And I listed them rapidly, in order of gravity: first the footling ones like laziness and forgetting to say evening prayers, then the medium ones like meanness and greed, and then – crash! and it came out truly like a heavy piece of ammunition – the cannonball of (what was it Reverend Mother had called it?) self-abuse, that was right, self-abuse.

There was a moment's silence after I had named the dreaded name. I could feel the waves of the poor man's embarrassment wafting towards me through the holes in the grille. Then, head and voice both suddenly very low, he cleared his throat and asked, 'Er, yes, child. That is a grievous sin indeed. And how many times have you committed it?'

I was silent while I consulted the piece of paper I was holding in my hand. The sum had been tricky to work out, but I had acted on the principle that it was better to over-confess than under-confess. Every Catholic knows that a deliberately unmentioned sin is an unforgiven sin. So finally, after calculating the yes-nights and the no-nights, and the twice-a-nights which invalidated the no-nights, I had arrived at a basic yearly average of 300. This I had then multiplied by the number of years (so far as I could remember, because the habit stretched back into the mists of early childhood) during which I had unwittingly indulged in this abominable practice. The product came out at 3,900, which, still following the above principle of abundance, I now quoted as a round 4,000.

There was another silence. Then a dull 'clunk' as Father Crispin's head, raised suddenly in what I imagine was an intolerable soaring of his embarrassment, hit the back of the confessional. Or perhaps I am wrong, perhaps it may have been in a deliberate effort to stun himself and find escape. I had to prompt him for my absolution, and yet again for my penance: with the blow he seemed to have forgotten his lines. 'Penance?' he murmured in a lifeless, faraway voice. 'Ah, yes, penance. Say two rosaries, ten "Our Fathers", ten "Hail Marys".' Then, in afterthought, but with a sudden return of vigour, waving his hands behind the grille as if chasing away a bat or a mangy dog, 'Go in peace, your sins are forgiven. Go, go, go!' It seemed, and still seems to me today, a remarkably cheap price to pay for 4,000 mortal sins.

I suppose I already knew that that was the end of things between Father Crispin and myself, but for the fortnight or so that remained until the end of term I continued to hope for an invitation to the cottage.

It never came. In a way I did not mind: I had my nice clean soul to comfort me, and also the certainty of having done a brave and righteous thing. Exams began, too, and gave me little time for regrets. But occasionally, when I saw the hunted, trapped expression in the poor man's eyes as he turned to face his all-female congregation during mass, or saw him flinch as he prepared to deliver communion to the row of open mouths and pink protruding tongues, then my certainty of having done the right thing would desert me, and I would begin to wonder whether by my confession I hadn't merely added one more involuntary sin to my grand total of 4,000: that of confirming a lonely old bachelor in his worst suspicions and frightening him out of his wits.

9

The Italian Finish

I don't know whether any of these establishments still exist today, if there is any demand for them, and if so on what lines they are run and what they are called. In the fifties, which is the time I had my dealings with them, they were called 'finishing schools'. The rationale behind the term being, I think, that they were supposed to bestow a kind of carpenter's finish on their pupils, not an executioner's or a bullfighter's. 'Polishing schools', then, would perhaps have made a better name. Or 'polishing places', seeing that the scholastic component in all cases was virtually nil. (Which is not the same as saying that the *educational* component was nil, oh, no, not at all.)

It was of the essence of such select and sought-after establishments that they did not advertise. Parents were meant to feel gratified simply by knowing the name: if you had heard of Madame So-and-so's in the Château country, or Madame Something Else's in Paris, or Contessa Thingimijig's in Florence, then you knew you were in the right swim, attuned to the right grapevine. The knowledge constituted, as it were, one of your badges of caste. You wrote or telephoned the school timidly but with a trace of pride, citing your contact, airing your own execrable French or Italian, hardly daring to mention fees. Not, I am Mr X, and I have decided to send you my daughter, but, I am Mr X, the friend of Mr Y (better still, Lord Y, or the Marquess of Y) and I hope you will take my daughter. This was what you said.

Yes, hope. Because a second characteristic of these places, logically tied to the first, and brilliantly engineered so as to pre-empt judgement on things like food and sanitation and sleeping arrangements and curricula, which were usually fairly shoddy throughout, was that *they* were the ones who did the choosing. You had found them out and shown them your badge, thus passing the first test of qualification, but the badge could then be stripped from you cruelly by a refusal, and you could be out on your ear among the riff-raff in a trice. It may seem strange – that membership of the class you aspired to or assumed to belong to in your own country, I mean, could be confirmed or revoked like this by some unknown foreign woman on the other end of a telephone line – but that's pretty much how it was. Madame, or la Signora or whoever, could demur, play for time, even postpone a candidate's attendance for a term or two because of lack of room, but if she came out with an unqualified no, then the verdict was damning: it was social failure, and of a particularly ignominious and riling kind. After this, the only resource for the family was to put about stories of their daughter's wickedness and rebellious spirit, so as to shift the emphasis from the social territory on to the moral one and to imply that the refusal on the part of the school was merely prudential. 'They didn't dare have her' was admissible, just. But the manoeuvre entailed risks of its own on the home front and was not willingly adopted.

Much to the inward relief of my parents (it would have been a solecism to betray pleasure or surprise), when they nerved themselves to apply to a small number of these so-called finishing schools on my behalf I was provisionally accepted by no less than five – two in France and three in Florence. Final acceptance, of course, in each case was still subject to what was called a 'visit of approval', another cleverly phrased term intended to imply that the school still had the faculty of turning me away if they didn't like the look of me, but nonetheless my parents were now miraculously placed on the choosing side, if only for a moment, and proceeded happily to effect their choice. With scant regard for mine, but that was only natural: university, when it wasn't for men, was for egg-heads and bluestockings and viragos and other weird and unmarriageable females *manquées*, and they didn't want to hear me talk about it. Ever again.

Coming down after about two and a half minutes of strenuous thought in favour of Italy (the French 'finish' was notoriously more expensive to apply and some said it chipped off quicker too), they then fitted me out with what they considered a suitable set of clothes for my interview – a prickly grey tweed suit with matching hat, if I remember rightly, plus Aertex shirt and moccasins; procured me a no-nonsense, anti-molester hair-cut at the local barber's, and packed me off to Florence in the company of an aunt to try my luck. A daughter's education warranted a trip to Italy on their part perhaps in theory, but not in practice, and definitely not during the flat-racing season.

'They may do the lettuce test on you,' my mother whispered urgently as the train was leaving, by way of final and only advice. 'That's what they did to poor little Judith Spence. Gave her a lettuce in a glass, and nothing but a teaspoon to eat it with. If they do, darling, then remember: anything is all right except trying to battle through with the teaspoon.'

What world did they live in, these parents of mine? What world did they think they were preparing me to face? Or did they not think of these things at all? Difficult to say.

My aunt and I arrived in Florence three days later and set about our visiting. It was nearly Easter, and very hot, and very dusty, and, to me at least, very, very strange. In the sense of foreign, I mean, more than odd; I could see almost at once that the place had a kind of inner harmony to it, if only I could make it out.

Our first call was on a certain Contessa Brizzi, I think it was, or it may have been Brazzi, directress of the choicest establishment of the three. My memories over the years have grown a bit hazy, but the impressions I have retained are of a dark, shuttered apartment somewhere in the middle of the city, with lots of stairs to reach it and very dingy furniture inside covered with cat-hairs and nail-varnish, and of sipping tea in this uncongenial setting with a handsome, managerial woman in her late-fifties with ice-blue hair and ox-blood nails, and being asked a great many questions. There was no lettuce served for tea, but I could see that my feeding habits were indeed under some kind of scrutiny. If it was delicacy the woman was after, then it struck me that this was not a good way of sorting English sheep from English goats, but I did what I thought was expected of me and foddered myself with unusual care, swallowing between sentences, speaking between swallows.

My behaviour and answers must have met with approval, and the Contessa's tone from inquisitorial turned flirtatious, almost wheedly in the end. My aunt was consequently more debonair on our next visit, going so far as to say, when the Signora Marozzi, or Gozzi, or Strozzi, or whoever it was on this second occasion, kept us waiting for a good ten minutes before putting in an appearance, 'Well, talk about manners. Who do they think they are, anyway, these greasy-skinned old Ferragamo bags?' She evidently felt herself on firmer ground.

After the second grilling, similar to the first in almost every way, except that the Signora Marozzi-Gozzi-Strozzi served coffee in place of tea and aimed her questions chiefly at my aunt (having perhaps spied on us during our wait and overheard the remark about the skin and the bags), we were practically, as my aunt put it, on the pig's back. Two of the best finishing schools falling over themselves, almost, to have me. What more could a girl want?

She rang my parents that evening to tell them the good news and then joined me in the dining-room of the *pensione* with a smile on her face: all settled. Tomorrow we would visit school number three – not that we needed to really any more, but it seemed a shame not to do the lot now that we had come all this way – and then we would make up our minds. Quietly. At leisure. While we went on a little shopping spree to the Ponte Vecchio to see if we couldn't find some nice plain silk ties and handkerchiefs for Uncle Boofy: English patterns were so loud nowadays. Oh, wasn't I lucky. Oh, didn't she wish she was my age. To be finished off in Florence – in this wonderful city, with all its wonderful frescos and whatnots. Wasn't I *thrilled*? Wasn't I over the moon?

I was not thrilled, I was downcast. I craved knowledge, I suppose, pretty blindly still in those days, only dimly aware of what the object of my craving was. Barring university, which was where I had heard talk of it being located, I didn't know where to begin to look for it, nor, for that matter, was I at all sure I would recognize it if I came across it. What I could instinctively recognize, however, from long familiarity with the flip side of the coin, was what it didn't look like and where it wasn't. And my brief visits to the establishments of Brizzi and Gozzi were enough to tell me that these were two just such places: whatever it was I was after – and as I say, my ideas on this head were vague – there was clearly none of it to be found in either.

It was only grudgingly, therefore, that I climbed into the taxi with my aunt the next day and allowed myself to be taken for my third and final test: this time at the house of a Signora Kesich, who ran, and had apparently run for many years, an august institution known as the Florentine Academy of Studies for Young Ladies. The Academy was famous for its site, a villa in the hills near Fiesole, and for the status of its ex-pupils, several of whom were rumoured to be royal. Rumour also had it that just recently poor Signora Kesich had begun, very, very slightly, to lose her grip. But this piece of news, said my aunt, had come to her from Molly Shannon, whose daughter had only just managed to scrape into a miserable cooking school in Devon, and might easily, therefore, not be true.

It was late afternoon when we reached the villa (the enthralling pursuit of my uncle's haberdashery having taken precedence on the agenda and occupied almost our entire day), and when the taxi-driver opened the door of the car to let us out a smell of flowers whooshed in, so thick and solid that it seemed to take up space, literally to invade the cab and force us out. My aunt sniffed and smiled, she was fond of flowers.

We paid off the driver, arranging to the best of our ability for him to call back for us in an hour, and then stood for a while in front of the gate, uncertain what to do. There was no bell, no nameplate, no latch even, just a number scrawled on the gate-post, and even that was half hidden under swags of creeper.

Everything looked very shut, very quiet, very inviolate. We cleared aside some of the foliage, just to make certain the taxi had brought us to the right place: sure enough, the number corresponded to the address we had been given. So taking courage we pushed open the creaky wrought-iron gate, snapping more tendrils of creeper as we did so, and made our way up an uneven stony path that led to the main doorway.

'Mmm,' sighed my aunt, sniffing again hard. 'Nice. I wish I could get my jasmine to grow like that.'

The door of the villa was ajar, revealing nothing but darkness beyond, and across the threshold, its shoulders hunched sharply like a wolf's, lay a large white dog which curled its lip at our approach and laid back a pair of tick-encrusted ears in warning. I checked my step, but my aunt, a staunch believer in canine perfection, noticed nothing amiss, and with a 'Sweetie, sweetie' and a string of loud-blown kisses into the air, stepped blithely over the animal's back and into the house, drawing me behind her. 'Good sign,' she said, 'a dog around.'

The dog and the jasmine were not the only signs
that met with my aunt's approval. No sooner were
we inside than we were met in the hall (more by
chance it seemed to me than design because I saw
the woman start a little when she saw us) by a gnom-
ish old housekeeper carrying a huge pile of linen,
who proceeded to fuss over us in a homely and
flattering way, long out of fashion among English
domestics: 'Le signore inglesi!' (The English ladies.)
'La signorina!' (That was me.) 'La mamma!' (My aunt.)
'Belle! Carine! Brave! Vengano, vengano.' (Come this
way, come this way, she would call Signora Kesich
immediately.)

'Pure Tiggywinkle,' my aunt whispered happily, as
we followed the old woman down a long, dark passage-
way and into a shabby, time-abused drawing-room as
pregnant with ruin as the set of a Chekhov play.
'Wouldn't I just love to have someone like that at
home. I bet she irons all those things with a flat-iron
too, and then pops them into a chest with lavender-
bags. Oh, look!' – our eyes were gradually becoming
accustomed to the gloom – 'Wellington boots. Riding
macs. Binoculars. And isn't that a shooting-stick I
see? How cosy, how very un-Italian. *What* a nice
atmosphere for a school. I wonder if Kesich could be
an English name in origin?'

Possibly the late Mr Kesich was at the bottom of
all the reassuring point-to-point clutter, and possibly
he did have English connections, I never discovered,
but the Signora herself, who now came into the room

to greet us, her hand in that of the housekeeper who appeared to be sustaining her and priming her with last-minute information on our account, was paradigmatically Italian. She was small and neat and impeccably dressed, with Cinderella-sized shoes and a grey tweed suit, which although technically like my own was at the same time so different that it might have come from another world. Beneath the suit she wore a shirt, tailored like a man's, but of silk as soft and creamy as a gardenia petal. A black velvet riband encircled her neck in a defiantly antiquated style, setting off the blackness of her eyes and eyebrows and the one-time blackness of her chignoned hair, and in her free hand she held an ebony walking stick. A slight smell of mothballs indicated that the clothes were not perhaps worn very often, but what was this when they were worn to such effect? Her elegance was timeless, borderless. A twelfth-century Russian peasant would have recognized it, a Maori warrior of the eighteenth, a London punk of the twentieth. A caveman or a space-man. Even, maybe, a fashion-conscious chimpanzee.

My aunt, in her way a more refractory target than any of the above, was captivated at once. Although I think the sight of the many signed photographs scattered around the room, featuring crowned and tiaraed ex-pupils of quite quenching grandeur, may have done something to soften her mood. I noticed none of the defensiveness she had shown with the other two directresses, none of the prickle, none of the hauteur, none of the nervousness either. I won't say she curtsied as she introduced herself, because her career in the saddle had warped her abilities in this field, but she sort of bent forward in eager submission, nudging me to do the same.

I noticed scarce inclination to criticize either. To me there was already something slightly awry in the Signora Kesich and her Academy for Young Ladies, a tiny, scarcely perceptible crack or flaw in the composition of both, but my aunt seemed unaware of it. And her unawareness deepened when a tray loaded with sweet wine and biscuits was brought in (two things she normally declared she hated) and she began dunking the latter in the former and tucking them away with gusto, following our hostess's example.

I sat there while she and the Signora chatted on to one another happily – chiefly about the exalted figures in the photographs and what they had been like in their young days when their human status was still visible – listing in my head the things I would draw her attention to afterwards. The way the faithful Tiggywinkle hovered over her employer, for example, reminding her time after time of my name:'Psss! Zoë, Signora, this one is a new one, she is called Zoë.' Reminding her, too, sometimes, if I fathomed the Italian correctly, of the actual purpose of our visit. The curious detail of the creeper binding fast the gateway, when surely the gateway ought only fairly recently to have been in constant use. The absence, too, of any sign of other pupils, save for the photographs. True, it was holiday-time and the other two schools had also been empty in this respect, but there I had at least noticed traces of occupancy by people of my own age – the stains of nail-varnish on the furniture, for instance, the odd record left lying about, the odd exercise book, sheets of jazz music on the piano. Here there was nothing, only the mounds of perished gumboots and fraying mackintoshes, and a tennis racket the shape of a Dali clock which couldn't have seen play in years. And lastly, if these things were not enough to stir my aunt's suspicions, there were the photographs themselves: image after yellowing image of regal young women in Fabergé jewellery, volunteer nurses in veils and bonnets, debutantes with fans, and frizzy fringes, and ostrich feathers in their hair. Not a portrait with even a remotely post-war flavour to it; not a sitter among them who could be still in her twenties today.

I looked around me to see if there was anything else I could add to my list. Signora Kesich, mistaking this for impatience reached out for my hand and stroking it with great sweetness said that perhaps . . . What-was-my-name . . .? ('Zoë, Signora,' prompted the gnome for a tenth time, hissing the sibilants through the gaps in her teeth in a spray of saliva.) Yes, well, perhaps Zoë was getting bored with all this gossip and would like to open up the french window at the far end of the room and take a little stroll around the garden? There was quite a big garden at the back of the villa, and I might find her niece there: she was often in the garden at this time of evening. That would be nice for us both. She, her niece, that is, was (another rapid hiss from the gnome, and the Signora's beautiful low voice which had begun to waver slightly towards the end of this speech retrieved its firmness) . . . was a teacher in the school, that was right, a teacher in the school. She would be my teacher.

Chronic vagueness, I noted in my mind, as I prised open the french window as instructed and stepped through it into the garden. The Signora Kesich, not to put too fine a point on it, was chronically vague. Possibly dotty. Possibly quite, quite mad. I was prepared for my parents' sake to spend a certain number of months cooped up in one of these fatuous places, biting my nails and smoking and growing fat and learning pidgin Italian and a smattering of art history or whatever, in the clutches, to use my aunt's phrase, of a greasy old Ferragamo bag, but I was damned if I would let myself be handed over to an out-and-out lunatic. No matter how sweet-natured, no matter how grand, no matter how well dressed. I hoped my aunt would see eye to eye with me over this, because, as I say, I could tell she was already very taken by the present set-up and leaning heavily towards it and away from the other two.

If she had seen the garden, it might have righted her balance for her, even without the aid of the scene that was presently taking place in it. My aunt was not one for tidy gardening, but she liked her plants, on a par with dogs, to be well tended, chatted up, given a lot of affection and time. This garden lay in a state of total abandon dating back years, perhaps decades – its paths cancelled by overgrowth, its flowers strangled by weeds, its beds parched, its trees and bushes drooping, its grass turned to a pampa of silvery, dusty hay. Like the Signora herself, it was possessed of an indestructible core or framework of elegance which still showed through in patches: in the quality of the roses, for example – some of them still hanging on to their blazonry, others already reverting to wild; in the presence here and there among the lashes of convolvulus, of a solitary peony, a throttled azalea bush, a branch of flowering magnolia; in the layout of the whole; in the perfect design of the Renaissance marble well that stood at its centre. But apart from these faint testimonials the garden's looks were gone, chased away by tares and parasites and simple long-term neglect. Although, again like the Signora its owner, in its decline it was still very striking.

The horticultural side of things, however, was not what interested me most. My attention was more for the well and the figures weaving round it – weaving round and round and in and out and back and forth, in such a state of absorption in what they were doing that, although I made no attempt to conceal myself and in fact even coughed quite loudly a number of times to signal my presence, they none of them heard me or saw me at all. Which was what, of course, emboldened me to go on looking.

Signora Kesich had said I might come across her niece in the garden, well, here she was. She stood beside the well, her back turned towards me, looking down into its shaft almost, although as I said, I don't think her eyes could have been focusing all that accurately: a tall, slim girl of about my own age, perhaps a few years older, with long sunburnt legs and no shoes on, dressed in a ragged, skimpy dress a couple of sizes too small for her, made of a wispy flowery material. The sort of dress that in England a charwoman might wear to work to save spoiling her better ones. Only on this girl it looked like a Paris original.

She stood motionless, the only one of the group to do so. The other figures, five of them, all dark young men in shirt-sleeves and flannel trousers with a faintly public-schoolboy look about them, circled round her in ever narrowing orbits of varying shape and speed, making strange grabbing movements with their hands as they went – at the hem of her dress, her ankles, her hair. When I began my observation they were still, I should say, about two yards away from her at the closest point, but they were drawing in fast. At first sight it looked like a kind of grandmother's footsteps played in a ring.

The girl did not turn round to check the advance of the other players, though, and this soon made me realize that the game was different. On the contrary, her body seemed actually to sway out slightly in a kind of languid pendulum movement and to invite their touches. The game was therefore *very* different.

One of the young men, I noticed, had a tie in his hand: most likely one of those quiet-patterned silk ties so dear to my Uncle Boofy. Each time he passed the girl he flicked out with it like a whip, as if trying to lasso

her. He flicked gently, precisely, aiming for the neck,
and when he drew close enough for the tie to touch
the girl's flesh I heard her laugh and saw her neck bend
towards it, again in a gesture of languid acquiescence.
Signora Kesich's niece was evidently enjoying herself.

I feared for her a little, I suppose. The young men
looked so set, so blind, so difficult to keep in check. I
was not close enough to see their eyes, but I imagined
them to be half closed, bleary, dopey almost. Even from
where I stood, from the heaving of their shoulders
and the sweat stains on their shirts, I could tell that
they were breathing hard and under some kind of
fierce inner pressure. What they would do when their
orbiting was complete and they had homed in on their
pliant centre of attraction, I did not know, but whatever
it was I judged that they would be single-minded about
it and difficult to deflect.

I stood and stared quite openly, secure in my
invisibility. The tie was lapping the neck regularly
now, almost within doubling distance. One of the
young men, smaller than the others and slightly
fairer-skinned, had caught hold of the hem of the
girl's dress in passing and lifted it well above her
knees. She laughed again and kicked his hand. He
put his hand to his lips where the kick had landed
and kissed it, half losing his balance, and only just
managed to reinsert himself in the quadrille without
being trodden on by the others. All the movements
now were very fast, very giddy-making, even for an
observer.

I was rapt, entranced, began to feel breathless myself. They were almost on her now. All five had mounted the first step of the base of the well, with only two steps to go before they reached her. The tie-flicker lashed out, encircled the neck, and caught the other end of his noose in his hand, drawing the girl's head towards him. The momentum of his companions carried him on, round to the far side of the well, but he held fast his silken cord until his head and that of the girl were almost touching over the well-shaft. Another of the participants rapidly took advantage of the girl's leaning position to plant a kiss on the back of her knee. I shivered. If I had been her I think I would have plunged down the well to get away from their pursuit.

Or would I? Signora Kesich's beleaguered niece turned briefly in my direction to deliver another kick to this new assailant and I saw that, even now, in the last desperate moments of her siege, she was still the one who wielded the power. I saw it in her eyes, in her smile, in her carriage. She was in command. Not quite in control, per-haps, because there was clearly no stopping the dynamics of the event she had set in motion, but in command. Power was hers and she knew it and relished it.

It was at this tantalizing point, just as the five had ascended the second step and were about to complete their orbit preparatory to mounting the last, that I heard my aunt calling for me. The hour had passed and our taxi had arrived. Something told me I had better answer her summons immediately, before she came out to look for me, and reluctantly I turned my feet in the opposite direction (doing my best to keep my head firmly where it was, although this was not easy) and began to walk towards the villa.

My vision of the finale was therefore sadly incomplete. *Opus interruptus* and curtain. The last thing I saw before I stepped back through the french window and into the darkness of the house was Tie-flicker, whose tie was now being knotted tightly in the small of his back by his companions, but whether around his own body alone in punishment, or binding his and the girl's body together by way of prize, I could not tell. I tended to think the latter.

My aunt sat complacently in the taxi on our way back to the city, exuding fumes of Marsala, while I looked at my tweeded reflection in the window and thought deeply and hard. After a while she spoke. '*Such* a nice woman, *such* a nice place. I don't think there is any question about which we plump for, Zoë dear, is there?'

'None,' I replied without inflection, my eyes still fixed on the mortified, ill-attired figure in the glass, 'none at all.'

'I thought not.' She relapsed into a happy silence and scuffed off her shoes. Her job was done, shopping and all. 'By the way,' she asked as we drew up in front of the *pensione*, 'did you meet the niece in the garden? What was she like?'

'I don't quite know,' I said, turning to face her and looking her honestly and squarely in the eye in the way I knew she liked. 'I met her, but we didn't talk much. I'm sure she'll turn out to be a very good teacher, though.'

My aunt fished for her shoes, wincing as she put them on, and patted my knee. I could see her mind was already straying to problems of meter-reading and correct tipping. 'And you a very good pupil, poppet,' she said in conclusion. 'And you a very good pupil.'

Of course, that went without saying: and me a very good pupil.

10

Camillo

So are the others, of course, but this is a *particularly* true story, one that happened just as I tell it: nothing added, nothing left out, nothing changed, not even the boy's name. I told it before once, at a dinner party, to a mixed reception. The man sitting next to me, a quicksilver Jewish lawyer from the States bent on pleasing, said that to him it was charged with deep psychological import, that it said in very little space a great deal about life and power and human relationships in general. He liked it immensely. Another man, sitting opposite, took a different stance and pronounced it an empty and discouraging piece of nonsense tending if anything towards the immoral. Both judgements surprised me and still do – to me the story is merely amusing. Although I suppose it's fair to say that it easily might not have been.

133

I was nineteen at the time, living with a rather frosty and stuck-up family of impoverished nobles in Milan, studying Italian and history of art. The first coat of finish having been applied and proved insufficient (and can you wonder?), this was the second – unfortunately of quite another hue.

I was a paying-guest, not an au pair, which put me so far as the family was concerned in an ill-defined position which I now understand they must have found socially irksome. Had they been able to order me around a bit in front of their friends, they would probably have had no difficulty in introducing me to them: I would have enhanced the family status and fitted in very well, and no doubt enjoyed myself too while I was about it. As it was, though, with the money flowing the other way, I was a faintly shaming appendage like a slow-witted child or a drunken uncle and they solved the problem as is common in such cases by segregating me almost entirely. When there were visitors the doors to the reception-rooms would remain firmly closed until they had left, and if the visitors stayed for lunch or supper my own meals would be brought into my bedroom on a tray.

Today, of course, having meanwhile got to know Italians better and learnt the extreme importance of the financial façade, or *figura*, which must be buttressed and sustained at all costs, I can see the reason for this cold-shoulder treatment and excuse it, but young and alone and vulnerable as I was then it hurt me deeply. So much so that even when there were no visits and the doors were left open, and signals were made that I was welcome to join the family in whatever it was they were doing, I would shake my head and shut myself into my room of my own accord. Eventually I hardly ever left it, save to go out for lessons, and this gained me a welcome but totally false reputation for bookishness and serious-mindedness: my absent presence among the guests could now be explained away easily, 'L'inglesina studia.' (The English girl is busy studying.)

I don't think I would have minded any of this particularly – the isolation, the loneliness, the leper's sense of unmerited but nonetheless branding shame – had I been allowed to keep it to myself. The head of the family, the Marchese, was tenderly polite to me when I met him on his own in the corridors, likewise his three elder sons: I could vaguely sense there was nothing personal or vindictive behind my exile. But I was not allowed to keep it to myself. The Marchese and Marchesa had a fourth son, Camillo, several years younger than the others: a boy of, what would he have been? six, seven, perhaps an undersized eight. Too young anyway to form part of the boycott agreement or to know on what foundations it was based. To him my position was one of weakness, pure and simple. He could smell my unhappiness, and the smell of it thrilled him. Bullied by his brothers and sat on by the maids, it must have seemed to him that at last a more insignificant member still had been added to the household, and he proceeded to capitalize on this unexpected piece of luck. The smallest pebble on the beach redeemed suddenly in its self-esteem by finding itself perched on an even smaller scrap of shingle.

The persecution, for such it was and both of us knew it, began gradually. At first the child would merely stand in the doorway of my room when it was open and stare at me, blank-faced and silent, until I shut the door on him. In my present state of pariahhood this in itself was unnerving enough. Next, always being careful to make sure no one else was around, he took to opening the door of his own accord and continuing his wordless staring-technique from just inside the threshold so that I was obliged to push him backwards across it before I could close the door. This went on for several weeks, with growing resistance on his part, and growing glee, the harder I had to push. Then things took another twist.

It seems absurd in retrospect that a normal, healthy and intelligent young woman of approaching twenty should allow her life to be made into a complete misery by a child less than half her age, whose methods of torture were on the face of it remarkably bland, yet this is exactly what happened. Despite my hard apprenticeship at school which you would have thought ought to have wised me up a bit, I made all the mistakes in the tormentors'-and-victims'-handbook. I suffered and I allowed my suffering to show. I bluffed, feebly and badly and far too late. I changed tactics, proffering friendship when it was no longer thinkable. I allowed myself to be drawn into physical contact with my oppressor, and when I used force I used just the wrong amount of it, only adding to the impression of weakness I had already made. I did everything wrong I could possible have done – partly, I suppose, because I was unwilling to admit to myself the seriousness of what was taking place.

The new twist I mention was this – and again it sounds deceptively bland in the telling: Camillo began using his voice. No longer content with silent provocation he would creep into my room at all hours, prop his head on the table where I was studying (or pretending to study, he knew as well as I did that my commitment was only sham) and, gecko-like, his water-coloured eyes staring out unblinking from behind pink-rimmed glasses, would chant at me in a thin little voice for as long as he could keep it up. Mocking, derogatory chants which, my Italian being what it was, I only half understood but whose tenor was nonetheless clear. 'Nge nge nge. Cacca, vacca, stracca, bislacca. Pazza, puzzi, cadi nel pozzo.' My own name would crop up frequently; he would spit it out with a grimace as if it tasted sour. I began, abjectly, to dislike the sound of it myself. Heaping error on error I would pretend to ignore his taunts, then ruin my pretence by swiping out at him and missing, then blush and laugh along with him half-heartedly, then try to bend my wits and my poor Italian to making up an insulting rhyme about him in retaliation. The most biting I ever achieved, I think, was 'Camillo, sporco grillo' (dirty grasshopper), which shows just how ill-equipped I was for this type of battle.

The afternoons, when Camillo was back from school and the others out or resting, soon became an authentic *auto-da-fé*: under the expert stimuli of my minute Torquemada I smarted, I writhed, I cast about in panic like a trapped animal that with every move embroils itself deeper in its captor's net. But I had my classes in the morning to distract me, and Camillo being packed off to bed early in the term-time, I had the evenings pretty well to myself. I managed. I tried not to think of my plight – as I said, I hardly acknowledged it anyway, so deeply did it shame me – and somehow or other I got by.

Then came the school holidays and a brusque stepping-up of rhythm in the torture sessions. Italian children on holiday, I discovered, have no bed-time and can roam unchecked by their elders until far into the night, provided they roam unobtrusively, which needless to say Camillo did. Unobtrusively, that is, as regards everyone else but me. The first evening I endured my punishment with resignation, I had been taken unawares. I pretended to read, refused to be drawn into the usual swiping and dodging match, tried to control my hands whose tenseness always gave me away, tried to look bored. As successfully as Joan of Arc might have tried to look bored at the stake: Camillo, like the crowd in Rouen, was not taken in.

The second night, however, I was waiting for him. Grimly, and for a change almost gladly, all other feelings – shame, embarrassment, inadequacy, self-disparagement and I know not what – having been suddenly replaced by anger, pure and simple. He may have sensed the change in me, for I remember him blinking in surprise behind his glasses for a second before I lunged out at him, but I didn't give him time to let the new information sink in. With fell precision I swept forward and grabbed him by the shoulder, yanking him round to my side of the table, then I took hold of arm and leg, lifted him off the ground and whirled him about me in a circle. The feeling was magnificent.

He weighed more than I expected, so that after a few orbits I was thrown off balance, and together we careered across the room in a kind of double dervish dance, faster and faster, more and more out of control, until with a dull, stodgy-sounding thud our revolutions stopped. The reason being, as I discovered when the blood-mist of my anger had subsided and I could see clearly again, that the boy's head had hit the radiator, thunk, bone against iron, bringing us up short.

He appeared to be dead, and indeed after such a blow it was hard to see how he could not have been. I sat over him pensively for a while, very clear-headed, totally unrepentant, watching the blood flow from the wound and the bruise swell like a molehill under construction. I regretted the inevitable fuss there would be with the parents when it came to explanations, but I regretted nothing else. Even when, after about five minutes or so, he showed signs of life and began moaning and groping around him for his glasses – shattered by the impact, as it turned out, and quite unserviceable – my attitude did not change. It would make little difference to the parents' reaction anyway, I reasoned, whether I had in fact succeeded in bashing their son's brains out or merely attempted to do so. Either way I had disgraced myself, either way my connection with the family, such as it was, was at an end.

In rigid silence I helped the child to his feet and mopped the wound for him. When the flux lessened I covered the mound with a handkerchief, led him round the room a few times to see if he could walk, handed him his pulverized glasses in an envelope, and then bundled him over the threshold as I had done so many times before (although this time with less impatience) and shut the door on him. Words were useless, and what could I say anyway that did not add to his triumph and make it all the sweeter? Dear Camillo, don't tell your parents *quite* how hard I flung you? Say it was a mistake? Say we were playing aeroplanes and you slipped? No, I scorned such measures, and I scorned to beg from the gecko. I did not even bother to remove the fragments of flesh and hair which I saw were still sticking to the radiator. Let them find them, I thought, who cared? However unintentional the actual dose of punishment, to me the little reptile deserved every ounce he had got.

I sat on the bed, waiting for the outcry. When none came I decided that perhaps Camillo had passed out again and would only do his reporting in the morning, so I began to pack my things, ready for departure. I

don't think I slept much, I was too anxious for the
scenes and the tears and the shouting to be over. Nor
did I spare a thought for Camillo and his concussion;
if he had survived that initial clash with the radiator,
I thought, he would survive anything. When morning
came I finished packing, folded up my sheets and then
sat down on the bed again. I must have finally dozed
off, because I was aroused in the mid-morning by the
maid, asking me if I was ill or something and did I
want a little late breakfast before she cleared away.

By now I had begun to sense something unusual in
the air, or let us say something so usual that it disconcerted me, and I remade my bed and pushed the packed
suitcases underneath it. Cautiously, my eyes and ears
very alert, I left my room and entered the dining-room.
There were used coffee cups and crumbs of brioche
everywhere – the family had evidently breakfasted in
the normal way and gone about their business. And to
reinforce this cheerful air of unconcern, there, sitting
at the head of the table hugging a mug of chocolate,
his spare glasses misted over by its fumes, a bandage
as big as a eunuch's turban covering half his head, was
Camillo himself.

Before I had time to say anything the maid came
in behind me with fresh coffee which she set on the
table, and ruffled his hair affectionately – what little of
it protruded from the bandage. 'E caduto poverino,'
she said, smiling at me and making a kind of boxing
gesture with her fists as much as to say, At least he *says*
that's how he did it – falling down – but more likely

he's been in a fight. 'Cade sempre.' (He's always falling down.) And still smiling she ruffled his hair again on her way out.

I looked at the child dispassionately, and he looked back. So he had not told on me. Well, well, well. For the first time I saw something faintly engaging about him: perhaps it was the spare glasses, they were a better colour than the others. Or perhaps it was the realization that by some mysterious jiggling of the figures our accounts were now settled to the satisfaction of both. I smiled at him, a polite, grown-up smile, and he responded. It was, we both of us knew it and acknowledged it accordingly, the turning-point in our relationship. Henceforth, from a respectful distance, speaking more to one another, maybe, but revealing less, we would be friends.

And so we were. I got used to my segregated life eventually, began to discover the pleasures of real study as opposed to pretended, and quite enjoyed the rest of my stay. Thanks to Camillo's discreet and patient coaching – he never again came into my room unless invited, and when he did he went out of his way to be charming to me – I also learnt splendid and fluent Italian which is with me to this day. That, then, is the story: true to the letter, in my view fortunately amusing, and with or without a moral as you care to view it.

AMANDA PRANTERA

THE SIDE OF THE MOON

It is A.D. 199 and Galen of Pergamos, former court physician and wily old bird, broods over the murder of his protégé, the emperor Commodus – officially portrayed as a sadistic, incestuous monster. Here Galen unravels the thread of lies, revealing the real, far more fascinating story of Commodus' life and death. Artfully wrought, witty and eloquent, this mesmerising recreation of Roman history lays bare the tissues which compose the 'truth'.

'Prantera's elegant novel is more than an attempt to rewrite the record on Commodus. It is about history and truth, and about the secrecy and misrepresentation that go hand in hand with totalitarian regimes and high-level court politics'
Times Literary Supplement

'Amanda Prantera has a liking for the stylishly off-beat . . . Her teasing novel converts one of the most cut-and-dried episodes of ancient history into a complex and shady business'
London Review of Books

'There can be no fear that the English novel is getting stuck in a rut when new young writers like Amanda Prantera can be found'
Evening Standard

'Here is an eerie original talent that keeps us on the hook'
The Guardian

FRANK RONAN

THE BETTER ANGEL

At seventeen, John G. Moore was in need of salvation. Afraid of the dark and of inheriting his mother's madness, he found irresistible the arrogant assurance of a newcomer to his Irish country school – the eccentric Godfrey Temple. Then John G. began to notice the cracks in Temple's patina. Tracing their volatile, doomed friendship, this powerful narrative captures the wit and anarchy of youth and the often painful transition to maturity.

'As exceptional as its predecessors . . . Ronan is as gifted as anyone from his generation, probably even from the next one up. His prose, understated and fluid, provides consistent and enormous pleasure; his exposures of the human heart are performed with a surgeon's skill and patience'
The Sunday Times

'Excellent . . . something of an Irish LE GRAND MEAULNES'
GQ

'Written in a limpid precise style that's resonant but never overwhelming . . . Ronan paints the understated anguish of his characters with wit . . . A mesmerising rites-of-passage story'
Time Out

'Marked by an eloquent and generally taut style . . . Ronan is excellent in tracing the relationship between the awkward and late-developing John G. Moore and the friend he hero-worships'
The Sunday Tribune

NIGEL WATTS

WE ALL LIVE IN A HOUSE CALLED INNOCENCE

James is turning thirty, stuck in the dismal routine of a librarian's job and a long-term relationship with his girlfriend. Then a human hand-grenade explodes into his life in the shape of Tad, a gay wheelchair-bound writer of pornographic stories. Before James knows it, he has an outrageously uninhibited new friend who goads him to take a fresh look at life, dispense with guilt and put his sexual fantasies into practice. For James, it's the first dangerous step on a journey into himself that could lead anywhere.

'The most moving, tender and funny exposé of a sexist creep I've ever read . . . a LUCKY JIM for the '90s'
Time Out

'Utterly likeable . . . James Morrison's interior life is portrayed with uncanny skill, a melange of sexual speculation and frantic observation of the world around him'
The Times

'A right shocker and a real corker for the Nineties . . . Watts clearly has the ability to play a variety of roles with outlandish elegance'
Daily Mail

'Watts has psychologically stunning insights and empathy . . . wise and moving'
The Sunday Times

'Gives a rare insight into male insecurity'
Today

ELAINE FEINSTEIN

LOVING BRECHT

A Jewish cabaret singer in Weimar Berlin, Frieda Bloom begins a love affair with the young Bertolt Brecht, only to find she is one of several women whose talent and emotions fuel Brecht's creative energy. In an effort to free herself from his spell Frieda marries, yet throughout the terrying events that follow – driving her from the Nazis to Stalinist Moscow and on to McCarthyite America – Brecht continues to exert his dangerous magnetism.

'Painfully acute, passionate, highly readable, delicately written'
Fay Weldon in The Times

'Brecht's presence – dirty, sexy, obsessive, charming, exploiting – is brilliantly constructed from Frieda's mixture of sexual passion and shrewd observation . . . This book is a work of art, quiet, elegant and deep'
A. S. Byatt in the Evening Standard

'An extraordinarily moving exploration of the way women give themselves without knowing why . . . an excellent novel'
Tania Glyde in The Times

'This enjoyable and surprisingly straightforward novel is the kind that gives faction a good name . . . most impressively, her evocations succeed in making well-worn historical events seem bewildering and real'
Claire Monk in the Literary Review

'A model of traditional storytelling excellence: lean, controlled and vividly imagined'
Jake Michie in the Daily Telegraph